THE OATH

A #WHYCHOOSE ROMANCE

T.M. Richardson

To Muses and Fantasies

CONTENT NOTE

Hello Lovers,

This novel is an erotic #WhyChoose romance, meaning, our main character doesn't have just one love interest. This is also an MMMF romance. That isn't a trigger warning, just a preamble. There will be a HEA, no doubt.

Trigger warning: cancer, death, divorce, (almost) sexual assault, kink and light BDSM, and drug use.

"If brothers dwell together, and one of them dies and has no son, the wife of the dead man shall not be married outside the family to a stranger. Her husband's brother shall go into her and take her as his wife and perform the duty of a husband's brother to her."

— DEUTERONOMY 25:5 (ENGLISH STANDARD VERSION)

THE OATH

1

AN UNUSUAL REQUEST

The beeping from the oxygen machine jolted Tatum out of her stupor in her study. She sighed, putting down her pen and closing her checkbook that she'd been attempting to balance for the past hour. She'd sent the nurse home hours ago, assuring her she'd be fine and could do this on her own. Now Tatum regretted that.

Tatum slowly opened the French doors leading to the playroom-turned-hospice room. The walls were still painted a faint gray blue, a leftover from the days when their son Morgan played with building blocks on the plush tan carpet. Morgan was a man now, a junior at Morehouse who was the spitting image of his father. Well, what he used to look like. Tatum looked at her husband. Franklin had been the most handsome man—broad, tall, with arms that were pure muscles and brawn. His round cheeks were now sunken in, and his clear, pecan-colored skin was sallow. He was a ghost of the man that he used to be.

"Honey?" Tatum slowly approached the bed. His body shook violently with each cough, rattling the rails of the hospital bed. Every cough made Tatum shudder, knowing that it shot nothing but fiery pain through Franklin's body. Franklin looked over in Tatum's direction and smiled.

At least his smile is still there, she thought.

"Hey, beautiful." Franklin reached out his hand toward Tatum, who'd taken a seat at her husband's bedside. Tatum intertwined her fingers with her husband's, his wedding ring now loose on him. She lifted his hand, gently kissing his knuckles.

"Hey, handsome."

"You ain't got to lie, Craig," said Franklin, another coughing fit muffling his laugh.

Tatum frowned. "Quit trying to make jokes, Frankie. Seriously." Tatum handed him a tumbler of water with a straw, motioning for him to drink.

After taking a few sips, he sighed. "I just want to make you smile. You don't smile these days, baby."

"What reason is there to smile, Frankie?" Tatum smoothed out his blankets, making a mental note to change the sheets tomorrow.

"Stop it, Tatum. I told you, there is plenty to smile about. We have a beautiful home. Raised a strong, Black man. Every day that I get to wake up and see you is reason enough to smile. We need to appreciate what time we have left."

Every time Franklin talked like that, Tatum felt sick. The entire ordeal had been unfair. Franklin didn't smoke, and he barely drank. The diagnosis for Franklin's lung cancer was grim. They'd given him six months. Seven, at most. Franklin had exceeded expectations when he hit the eight-month mark. Now, in month thirteen, things were taking a turn. It was only a matter of time. Tatum wasn't ready for it.

Franklin pushed the button on the bed and raised up his head. Instinctively, Tatum got up to fix his pillows, but Franklin shooed her away.

"I am fine, Tate. Stop fussing over me."

She gave a weak smile. "It's my job to fuss over you."

"We pay people to do that, Tatum."

"Yeah, but I'm your wife…"

"When have we ever done that bullshit?" Franklin interrupted. "My wife? You're also your own person."

Tatum bit her lip, embarrassed. Frankie was right. They'd never done the whole "gender roles" thing in their marriage. Why was she starting now?

"Babe, when is the last time you went shopping? Caught a movie? Had brunch with your girlfriends? Regardless of what's going on with me, you need a life, my love. "

"I have a life, Franklin. But you…"

"I am not your life, Tatum. I never was. Not now. Never."

Tatum's lips parted and then she quickly closed them. "But what if I go out and then…" She stopped. She didn't want to think about that.

Franklin shrugged. "Then you miss the worst part of it all. Maybe I don't want you to see it."

Tatum's eyes welled up with tears. "No. I need to be here. I need to." In the twenty-two years of their marriage, they'd rarely been apart. There was no way she'd not be there when he transitioned.

"You've seen enough. You've seen my hair fall out. You've seen the chemo and radiation make me sick. You've suffered enough, my love. I give you permission to have some fun."

Tatum shrugged. "Fun? I can't have fun without you." And who would want to have fun with her now? She was terrible company for anyone. All she did was worry about Franklin. Her mind could literally focus on nothing else.

"Baby, yes you can. That's something you're going to have to get used to doing, anyway."

Tatum sighed. "I guess."

Franklin's fingers slowly rubbed Tatum's arm. She looked at him, his eyes lingering on her lips. Even in his weakened physical state, he melted his wife with just his touch.

"Tatum, can I ask you something?"

"Anything."

"When's the last time you touched yourself?"

Tatum's eyes widened. "What? Why?"

She hadn't thought about sex or anything remotely sexual for the past year since Franklin's diagnosis. They hadn't made love in months, not since the cancer got worse. She remembered their last time with fondness.

It had been amazing. It was as if Franklin knew it would be the last time he'd have the strength to touch her like that, so he gave the sexual performance of his life. She'd never orgasmed so many times. Tatum had soaked the sheets down to the mattress.

The faintest grin crossed Franklin's face. "You need some kind of pleasure in your life. I can't give it to you. Not like this. Remember all the fun we used to have? All the sexy shit we used to do."

A shiver ran down Tatum's spine as she thought about Franklin in healthier times. Their love life had never been an issue. No matter how broke they were, or how petty the argument, their sex life was something that never suffered. Sometimes they would fight over the smallest of things just to end up fucking like rabbits. It was a miracle they'd only had one baby instead of hundreds.

Tatum shook her head. "Frankie, honey, I don't have time to think about that. The medical bills are piling up. I'm on sabbatical from the university and I'll have to go back soon. I'll have to arrange your care, and Morgan may need things for senior year."

"Shh, beautiful. Morgan is fine. I just want you to think about yourself for a change. Something other than bills or me and this fucking cancer."

Franklin coughed, the sound reverberating in the room. Tatum reached for the oxygen, adjusting the nasal cannula for Franklin's comfort. Grateful, he inhaled deeply. His grip tightened on Tatum's arm, which forced her to turn and look at him. "Seriously, Tatum. Get the fuck out of this house. Have some fun."

Tatum sat on the edge of the bed. "And do what, Franklin?"

"Get your back blown out."

Tatum nearly fell over in shock. "Franklin! You are asking me to cheat on you!"

Franklin laughed. "Is it cheating if I know about it? Baby, I will not be here much longer. You and I know this. I am giving you permission to have a basic human need met."

Tatum shook her head. "Franklin, that is reckless. Besides, where the hell is a forty-something-year-old woman supposed to find a random man to screw?"

"What about Tinder?"

Tatum frowned. "Ugh, that's gross. What if one of my students finds my profile and swipes right?"

"Well, then they could fulfill their teacher/student fantasy," Franklin said with a smile. Tatum wasn't the least bit amused. At that moment, her cell phone buzzed in her pocket. It was Miles, Franklin's partner at the law firm and best friend. Grateful for the distraction from this conversation, she read the text.

MILES

Hey T. How's he doing?

Tatum looked up from the phone. "It's Miles."

Franklin nodded. "Tell him I'm not dead if that's what he's asking."

Tatum laughed, then shot off a text.

TATUM

He's good. Told me to tell you he isn't dead yet.

Miles quickly replied.

MILES

> Still an asshole, though. Well, do you mind if me and the boys come over and watch the game with him?

Tatum scratched her head. Franklin needed to rest but she also could use a bit of a break. Especially from the conversation they were having.

TATUM

> How many of ya'll are coming over? I can order wings or something.

MILES

> Just me, Cassidy, and Deacon. And don't worry about the food, T. We got it. Just want to spend some time with our boy. Check in on you too.

Tatum smiled. Miles and Franklin had started their firm fresh out of NCCU law school, and with a lot of hard work, had turned it into a successful practice. Their friend Deacon joined the firm later as a forensic auditor, overseeing some of their larger cases. And Cassidy… Well, Tatum wasn't sure what Cassidy did.

He was aloof, not saying much around her. But he was a nice guy and had his shit together. The guys often joked that was the "Tommy" of the group, because for the life of them, they did not know what he did for a living. They were all a handsome, accomplished bunch. Franklin was the glue that held them all together.

"Frankie, Miles wants to know if he and the guys can come and watch the game with you?"

Franklin nodded. "That would be cool. If they can put up with the coughing."

Tatum shot Miles a text, confirming that it would be fine if they stopped by. As she put her phone away, Franklin tugged at the bottom of her shirt.

"Remember how you'd get all dressed up in barely anything under your trench and we'd go to Secrets? We'd watch the other couples, get so turned on, and fuck all night."

Tatum swallowed, her nipples tightening at the memory. She hadn't thought about Secrets, the members-only swingers club, in years. Tatum and Franklin were more voyeurs than swingers, watching everyone's pleasure, which heightened their own. When they first began dating, they went often. Each time, they'd end up having some of the best sex of their lives. When they had Morgan, she and Franklin rarely visited, except for anniversaries or birthdays when they wanted to spice things up. They would role play or do some light kink. The last time they'd gone to Secrets, Franklin was as fit as a horse. Or so they thought…

"Frankie, I'd never go to a place like Secrets without you. Is that even safe?"

"Baby, there is security everywhere, you know that. Besides, you can meet someone and not have to worry about them disclosing to the world who you are. NDAs and all of that. Very discreet."

Tatum was becoming increasingly frustrated. "Franklin, you're asking me to break my vows. I just… I can't."

"I want you to go. And come back and tell me all about it. Don't leave out any detail."

"Frankie, I…."

"Tatum, do something for yourself. For me."

"Frankie, you're talking foolishness." Tatum rose from her spot on the bed, leaned down and kissed Franklin on the head. "I'm going to go tidy up before Miles and the guys get here. Get some rest so you can enjoy the game."

With that, Tatum closed the French doors and headed back to her office.

2

SHAMELESS

A lisa, don't just stare at me! Say something!"

Tatum watched as her cousin Alisa held her mimosa suspended in the air over her kitchen island.

"T, what do you want me to say? What kind of request is that for a dying man to make?"

"Right!" Tatum poured herself another mimosa. She peered out across the hallway at Franklin, who was sound asleep. "I can't do that. I can't break my vows that way."

Alisa nodded. "I understand totally. But then again, Franklin is asking you to do this. He's giving you permission to rekindle that dormant part of yourself. How long has it been, again?"

"It's been a year. Thirteen months, to be exact."

"Thirteen months of no loving? Not even touching yourself?"

Tatum shook her head. "I can't focus on that right now. I just want Franklin to…" Tatum dropped her head and pounded her fist against the counter, ignoring the pain that shot through her fingertips. "I know he's dying. I just want to be there. He can't push me away into some man's arms before he's gone. That makes no sense!"

Alisa frowned. "I don't think he's doing that, Tate. I think he just wants you to think about something else other than him."

Tatum bit the corner of her lips as she turned to place the empty juice carafe in the sink. She understood that was exactly what Franklin wanted her to do. How could she think about anyone else but him? For the past twenty-two years, she'd only slept with one man. The idea of stripping down for another terrified her. She was far from a virgin when she met Franklin, but she'd never thought about anyone else since then. Who would want her, anyway? She wasn't the Nubian goddess that Franklin fell in love with—young, fine, and tight. She had gray hairs, saggy tits caused by a breast-feeding Morgan, and a stomach that needed shapewear to look decent in anything. Not to mention, her pussy didn't get wet without the help of lube most of the time. She'd be a hassle to anyone looking to be pleased sexually.

She pulled the hash brown casserole out of the oven. "Lisa, no one wants to see me naked. I'm sure of it."

Alisa waved her hands. "Oh, please girl! You still got hips that won't quit, big titties, and a beautiful face. Someone is going to want you."

Tatum raised a brow. "I see you didn't mention my ass."

Alisa shrugged. "Eh. You aren't working with much in that department, so… Thank God you were blessed with a pretty face."

The clanging and thud of boots against the hardwood floors interrupted their cacophony of laughter. Tatum looked up at Cassidy, who was in a tank top, jeans, and boots, covered head to toe in soot.

Tatum clutched her beating chest. "Holy shit! Cassidy, you scared the crap out of me. I almost forgot you were here."

Cassidy smiled, wiping his hands on his jeans. "My bad, Tate. I didn't mean to scare you. I fixed that issue with the water heater. Anything else you need me to look at?"

Ignoring Alisa mumbling "her pussy" under her breath, Tatum shook her head. "No. Thanks! And you didn't have to do that!" Tatum reached into the fridge, handing him a bottle of water. She watched as he drank the entire sixteen ounces in three gulps. His Adam's Apple bobbed, and Tatum wondered if he consumed everything with fervor.

"It was no problem. When we came over last week for the game, I heard you complaining about the water not heating. I just saved you a couple of bucks and a service call."

Alisa leaned her hand on her chin. "Are you a handyman by profession, Cassidy?"

"Um, no," Cassidy said with a smile. "More like a jack of all trades, master of none. I'm going to peek in on Frankie, then I'll let myself out. I'll check in next week. Good seeing you again, Alisa."

Alisa waved her fingers in Cassidy's direction. "You too, hon. Don't be a stranger."

Tatum nodded. "Thanks, Cassidy. I appreciate it. I'll text you."

When Cassidy had turned down the hall toward the playroom, Alisa fanned herself. "Child, what I wouldn't give to mount that man! He is so fine. And so nice! Every time I see him, he's always a gentleman. All of Frankie's boys are so fine! I can't stand it."

"You're shameless," Tatum chided.

Alisa was right, though. Frankie's friends were handsome guys, but all very different. Miles was divorced, yet never talked a bad word about his difficult ex-wife, even giving her a hefty alimony payment because she'd helped him through law school. Deacon was a player, never settling down with anyone but very discreet and respectful. And Cassidy, well… Tatum didn't know a thing about his love life. If he was gay, straight, or whatever. He didn't bring women around them. He never talked about dates or any of that. He was just that secretive.

Alisa groaned. "I know. But he seems like such a good dude! The kind you make your man!"

"You trying to make him your man, Lisa?"

"Maybe just for the night." Alisa laughed as she drank her mimosa.

Tatum laughed as she wiped down the counters. "Yeah, you would do that."

Alisa leaned back, her arm resting on the back of the barstool. "And you all still don't know what the man does for a living?"

"I thought he was in finance, but I don't think so. I tried asking Frankie once and he said, 'it's probably a good thing we don't know.' Whatever he does, trust me, his normal attire isn't tanks, dirty jeans, and Timbs."

"Oooh! Maybe he's an assassin! Like Mr. and Mrs. Smith!"

"Or," Tatum interrupted, "maybe he's just private

and doesn't want folks in his business. Ever thought about that?"

"Girl, I guess. But back to your business. What are you going to do?"

Tatum blew out a breath. "I don't know, Lisa. Seems risky."

"Why don't I come with you? I mean, I've never been to Secrets before. It could be fun. Plus, we can keep an eye out for each other."

"It's members only, and it's really expensive."

Alisa folded her arms, indignant. "Okay? What are you trying to say? Because I'm a hairstylist, I can't afford it? I'll let you know that my weaves and installs could buy your house five times over. How much is membership?"

"The initial fee is ten grand, with a yearly fee of two. Wait, that was the price for couples. It could be more for single folks. I don't remember. I haven't gone in years."

"Shit! Are you fucking serious?" Alisa's eyes nearly bulged out of her head.

Tatum laughed. "I told you it was expensive. You don't have to do this, Lisa. Seriously, I don't even know if I should."

"Well, if you decide to go, I am going with you. Period."

At that moment, they heard the familiar sound of

the video doorbell chime, showing that someone had left through the front door. Cassidy disappeared without a peep. Alisa sucked her teeth, disappointed.

"Damn! He's gone just like that? I didn't even get my chance to go in for the kill."

Tatum laughed. "He'll be back. Trust me, you'll get your chance to mount him, cowgirl! Now, help me polish off this casserole and mimosas before Frankie wakes up."

"You already know! I got you, cuz!"

3

SECRETS

I t's good to see you again, Mrs. Simmons. I see that it's been a while. Will Mr. Simmons be joining you?"

"No."

Tatum nervously smiled at the concierge at the front desk of Secrets as the house music pumped through the speakers. She couldn't believe she was going through with this ridiculous plan, spurred on by the encouragement of her cousin, Alisa. When she told Franklin that she was heading out, honoring his wishes, he smiled happily and told her to go. She paid extra for a night nurse to tend to him, asking them to call her if there was an emergency. The sweet-faced nurse smiled and assured her she had it under control.

The attendant handed Tatum and Alisa tablets to

fill out personal information. Marital status. Last time they were tested for STDs. Could there be a possibility they were pregnant? If they had any food allergies, COVID exposure, and an NDA.

"Damn, girl, are they gonna ask me for a DNA sample too?" whispered Alisa as she handed back the tablet.

"They have to make sure things are legitimate. Secrets is pretty intense. Not to mention, you'll be surprised who you may run into here. Politicians. Ballers. Pastors."

"Whoa."

Tatum handed the attendant her credit card. "Ms. Williams is my guest for the evening."

"Very well. The total will be six thousand. Five thousand to reactivate your membership, and one thousand for your guest's one-night pass."

Tatum swallowed, tugging at the belt of her trench coat. With that amount, she could have taken a cruise or something. She and Franklin had been very smart with their money, but this was a foolish expense. Her sabbatical from the university would end. She had nurses and care for Franklin to think about. Yet here she was, spending it on a potential sexual excursion.

The attendant handed Tatum back her card and

pulled back the curtain leading to the main room. "Enjoy yourself, ladies."

They'd divided the main room into a dance floor, a second area for tables and chairs, and two massive wrap-around locations, one for a bar and the other for a buffet.

"Look, I know we came to get freaky, but a sista really could use a plate of prime rib," Alisa shouted over the music.

"I don't know if I can eat anything, but hey, do you. It's all included. Drinks too."

"Word? I am about to get fucked up. Let's get a drink!" Alisa tugged at Tatum's hand, leading her toward the barstools. The bartender, a shirtless, muscular, deep chocolate brother with dreads, came over to take their order.

"Ladies. You're looking good tonight. What can I get you to drink?"

"What about you?" asked Alisa, seductively. Tatum slapped her on the leg. "Ouch!"

The bartender gave a soulful laugh. "Sorry, ladies. I'm on the clock, so I can't partake in any fun."

"Oh well. Let me get a Crown and Coke on the rocks. My friend will have a glass of rosé."

"Got it."

"Girl, you need to chill! The attendants, servers, and security are off limits. You can't solicit them for anything, or you'll be out on your ass," Tatum whispered out of earshot of the bartender making their drinks.

Alisa frowned. "Sorry, sis! I didn't know the rules. You gotta school me."

"Yeah. Just...take it easy."

"Fine. But this is a kind of exciting! Just look around. All these half-naked people gyrating on the dance floor, making out at tables. Just...this is turning me on!"

Tatum looked around. They packed the dance floor with ladies in lingerie and sky-high heels and men in boxers and silky robes. A couple of women were making out in a booth as a pair of men watched. Tatum inadvertently locked eyes with a shirtless guy with nipple piercings that glinted under the strobe lights. His eyes bore into her, his erection visible in thin, white boxer briefs. His body, with its broad shoulders and taut muscles, reminded her of Franklin in healthier times. She had to look away. Tatum clinched her thighs and threw back her glass of rosé, signaling the handsome bartender for another.

"Damn girl! Slow down," Alisa warned.

"I can't. I'm nervous. Maybe this was a mistake, Lisa. Seriously. Maybe we should go home."

"Girl, we just got here. We haven't even gotten to

the good stuff. Listen, I'm going to go grab a bite to eat. You just take some deep breaths. I'll be right back."

Tatum watched Lisa saunter across the dance floor, her high ass barely covered by her satin slip dress. If anyone was going to have a good time, it was her cousin.

The bartender slid the cold glass of rosé in front of Tatum. "You okay?"

Tatum took a sip. "A little nervous. It's been a while since I've been here. Maybe I'm out of my league."

The bartender's eyes roamed over Tatum's body, landing on cleavage peeking atop her trench as he dried a rocks glass. "Trust me, you'll have nothing to worry about tonight, ma'am. Enjoy."

Tatum bit her lip, trying very hard not to blush. She couldn't remember the last time a man unabashedly checked her out.

She continued to sip her drink as Alisa returned to the seat next to her, a plate full of food in her hand. Tatum frowned. She could never fuck on a full stomach, but apparently Alisa didn't have those issues.

"Whew, girl! I got approached by a couple and two dudes just on my way to the appetizers." Alisa crunched on a cucumber. "You see anyone you like?"

Tatum shook her head. "No. I'm just taking it all in."

After Alisa polished off her plate of appetizers and two more Crown and Cokes, she was more than ready to head back to the private rooms. Tatum's stomach flipped with nervousness. Was she really about to do this? They approached the security desk near the locker rooms.

"Ladies, your phones, please."

Tatum and Alisa handed the security desk attendant their phones for a lock with an assigned number so that they could retrieve them at the end of the night. The lock also doubled as their security lock in the main room, where people disrobed down to their comfort level.

"Wait? Men are in here too? Dicks are swinging, girl!" Alisa was terrible at whispering. A few men chuckled in response.

Tatum looked around. Men of all shades of browns in various builds were naked. Her eyes dipped to a few exposed dicks. "Yes. It's unisex, Alisa. Please stop making it weird."

"And I don't have to get buck naked, right? I can keep on my bra and thong?"

"You can. But honestly, I don't want to see you naked."

"Hater." Alisa slipped out of her satin dress, down

to a sheer bralette and thong. "You've seen me naked plenty of times!"

"We were kids, Alisa. And speaking of naked, I really am not trying to see you get your back blown out."

"Then I suggest you turn your head, hoe!"

Tatum chuckled. "That's fair." She unhooked her trench, revealing a yellow bra and garter set.

"Ooh, that's nice!"

"Yeah. Franklin bought for it for me the last Valentine's Day before..." Tatum shoved her coat into the locker, along with her purse, slamming it close before placing the numbered lock on it. She shook her head, trying to forget about better days. "Let's just go out there and get this over with so I can go home."

Alisa and Tatum made their way out of the lockers toward the glass-encased rooms lining the walls. Porn was playing on the television as a red light glowed in each room. Alisa paused at a room where a man and two women were engaging in heavy foreplay. The couple was seated against the bench on the wall, her legs open wide as her head lay in the man's lap. She lazily darted her tongue at his dick as his hands stroked her clit. The other woman, curvier with braids that went down to her ass, was on her knees in front of the man. He held her by the braids as she sucked his balls. By the look on his face, he was in heaven.

"Damn, they look like they are having fun," remarked Alisa, her hands against the glass as she peered inside.

"You can go ask if they can include you in the fun."

"Nah, I don't wanna share a dude with another girl. I wanna be the center of attention."

Tatum chuckled. "Selfish as always, I see."

"Always."

They continued on, past another room that had a man tied up, arms and legs spread outward, mouth gagged as he reclined against the obedience chair. Another man was in the corner, jacking off as he watched a gorgeous woman with a blonde bob flog the man in the chair. Tatum couldn't take her eyes off the scene as the man jacking off, dick glistening with precum, appeared to be getting closer and closer to release.

"This is some freak shit," Alisa whispered.

"Shh." Tatum pressed herself against the window for a better view. She felt wetness pooling at her center. Franklin was never into heavy BDSM, no matter how many times she tried to convince him to try. The most he'd do was smack her ass or choke her a bit during sex. But she'd always wanted to be tied up. To be teased. To let someone else be in total control for once. Lately, she was tired of having to make all the decisions. What she wouldn't give to relinquish control over everything happening in her life right now…

Tatum shook her head. "Let's go." She took Alisa by the hand and walked toward what they called the Cloud Room. It was a massive space with nearly twenty California king beds and a ceiling painted to resemble the Sistine Chapel. When Tatum pushed open the French doors leading to the space, Alisa let out a gasp.

"They really getting it in in here!"

Guests occupied every bed with various shades of brown limbs and bodies, contorted into every sexual position. The sounds were like porn, only dialed up to the maximum amount of decibels. Couples of varying combinations were in their own world. Although no one was really looking at her, Tatum felt like she was being watched as she observed them. This was what she and Franklin liked to do. To watch. To get so turned on that they had to fuck the desire out of each other.

I shouldn't do this alone. I should be here with him, thought Tatum.

Alisa nudged Tatum back to reality. "T, I think

someone has eyes on you. 10 o'clock. And, uh, he's fine as hell."

Tatum looked in that direction and spotted the guy she'd seen earlier while sitting at the bar. This time, he sat on the edge of the bed as a woman gave him head. The woman gave her best performance, slurping up and down his dick, saliva—and maybe cum—coating it obscenely. His hands cupped her heavy tits as she did so. But his eyes stared straight at Tatum. It was unnerving.

Tatum watched as he whispered something to the woman. She stopped, got off her knees, wiped her mouth, and kissed the man's cheek, then moved down the row to another bed where a man beckoned her. The guy staring at Tatum then rose, pulled up his white briefs and began walking toward her.

"Girl, he is coming this way! Let me go. I see something I like, anyway. Have fun!"

"Lisa! No! Don't go," hissed Tatum, but it was too late. Alisa was gone, her attention grabbed by a very sexy Blasian guy covered in tattoos and nothing else. As she turned to monitor her cousin, Tatum was nearly face to face with her watcher.

Shit.

His honey brown skin and nipple bars glistened under the bluish hue of the strobe lights. He was tall, so much taller than Tatum had expected, and she had to strain to look up at him. He had a warm face. A youthful face. How old was he? As old as Morgan? She shouldn't have been thinking about her son at a time like this. Not when a man was standing in front of her in the tightest boxer briefs and some athletic slides. Tatum swallowed as her eyes traveled from his deep, brown eyes, across his broad shoulders and his chiseled chest, down the lines of his carved Adonis belt, and settling on one of the biggest dicks she'd ever seen in her life as he stroked it in front of her. It looked as long, thick, and wide as a prayer candle on her altar, and she definitely needed to pray.

"I saw you earlier," his voice boomed. "You're beautiful."

"Tha—thank you," Tatum stammered. "You are too."

His eyes traveled down the length of her body. "Are you here alone?"

"No. I am with my cousin. She is here…somewhere."

The stranger's eyes followed Tatum's hand as she ran it through her hair, nervously. "And your husband?"

Shit. Amid everything, she'd forgotten to take off her ring. "He's…not here," was all that she could say.

The young man's hand reached out and stroked

her arm. Goosebumps immediately pebbled her skin and her nipples stiffened through the sheer yellow fabric of her bra.

"He let your fine ass come out alone to play? Brave man. That's what's up…"

Tatum bit her bottom lip so hard she could taste her flesh becoming metallic. "Hmm. He did."

"So, do you want to play, lady? Because I'd love to play with you."

Tatum took some deep breaths. If she was going to do this, this man seemed like the right guy to do it with. He was beautiful, with a beautiful dick to match. She was sure that he could fuck her until she saw stars.

Before Tatum could give the handsome stranger an answer, she felt a hand tug her arm with force, pulling her away from the guy swiftly.

"Hey man! What the fuck!"yelled the beautiful stranger as he became smaller and smaller, nearly out of sight.

Tatum could hardly see in the darkened area where she was being led to. Her heart raced, and she feared the worse. Was she being attacked? She didn't have a weapon, but she tried to remember all the self-defense lessons she and Alisa had taken that summer at the Y. And where the fuck was security?

A door swung open, and they pushed her inside a

room. Tatum's eyes adjusted as the red lights glared off the stark white of the walls and bed, literally making it look like a portal to Hell. If she was going to die this way, at least she had on nice underwear.

"Go home, Tatum."

Tatum turned toward the commanding yet familiar voice. Her eyes adjusted to the full beard, full lips, and the gleaming bottom grill in her face.

"Cassidy? Why the fuck... Why are you here?"

"Go home," he repeated, ignoring her question.

Tatum folded her arms indignantly like a pouty teenager. "Don't tell me to go home! I'm an adult!"

"Go home, Tate. Now." Cassidy stepped closer to Tatum as she backed against the wall. She looked at his round, bearded face, which was usually quiet and kind, but now filled with unrecognizable rage. It scared the crap out of Tatum, which somehow made her nipples throb.

"Listen, if you think I am cheating on Franklin. I'm not... it's just..."

"I don't," he interrupted. "Just, go home."

Tatum looked at Cassidy, his face still angry. But then, her eyes traveled down from his round, familiar face, and plump lips, across the swell of his chest, covered in tattoos that seemed like hiero-glyphics, and down to the towel wrapped across his hips that did very little to hide an obvious erection.

Did he have a literal hard-on while bossing her around? Was this some kind of sick game?

Tatum stood still. "Tell me why I should go home?"

With that, Cassidy slammed his hand against the wall next to Tatum, pushing himself close to her face. She could feel the heat of his breath on her neck, and she winced.

"Tatum, I won't ask again. The next time I have to ask, I will drag you out of here." Tatum should have been angry at Cassidy for speaking to her this way. Her pussy said otherwise, throbbing with arousal and weeping with wetness. It was confusing.

Tatum trembled as Cassidy moved closer. "I am here with Alisa. What am I supposed to do? Just leave her here? I can't do that, Cass!" She didn't recognize her voice as she spoke. Who was she right now?

Cassidy leaned back, his eyes surveying Tatum's face as if to see if she was lying. Satisfied that she wasn't, he answered with a calmer tone. "I'll make sure she gets home. But for now, you need to go." With the other hand, Cassidy opened the door to the room slightly and nodded toward it. "Now. Leave."

Tatum said nothing as she backed out of the door as Cassidy slammed it in her face.

Terrified, Tatum went back toward the Cloud

Room to find Alisa, to tell her what happened and give her a heads-up that Cassidy was there. Thankfully, the young man who had approached her was gone. Tatum peered in the room, trying to find Alisa, but there were no signs of her. Tatum walked toward the pools and jacuzzis, only to find her cousin getting her pussy eaten out by the handsome Blasian guy from before, while another guy with blonde tipped dreads had his dick down her throat. Tatum closed her eyes and shook her head. Not an image she wanted seared in her brain. She had to go.

Tatum grabbed her things from the locker, quickly put on her coat, and retrieved her phone. Valet brought her car within minutes, and before she knew it, she was driving nearly eighty miles an hour on I-75. Cassidy had scared her beyond measure. What would he do? Would he find the guy who tried to fuck her and threaten him? Would he tell the rest of Franklin's friends that she was out cheating? It was a huge misunderstanding, one that Cassidy had refused to let her clear up. Instead, he just yelled at her to go home. And strangely, she had been too turned on to argue. It made no sense.

Tatum pulled up to the house and saw that most of the lights downstairs were on. It was nearly two in the morning, and Franklin should have been asleep—or at least trying to sleep. Tatum parked the car in the garage and took off her shoes at the mudroom, careful not to make any noise. In the kitchen, she saw the night nurse, Zora, on the phone. She looked up from her phone, wide eyed.

"Oh, dear God! There you are. Did you get my texts? I'd been texting you for an hour!"

Tatum looked at her phone. There had been a dozen texts from Zora. She hadn't been able to see them with her phone locked away in the club. "I'm sorry, I wasn't able to get to my phone. What is it?"

Zora shook her head. "Dr. Simmons, Mr. Franklin is taking a turn for the worse. His oxygen levels are pretty low, and he's really struggling to breathe. He was calling for you. I was going to call the ambulance, but I know you have a DNR in place. I wanted to be sure if…"

Before she could finish, Tatum rushed past Zora and down the hall into the playroom where Franklin lie in bed. His breathing was rougher than she'd ever heard it, and his chest was nearly concave as he exhaled.

"Frankie? Baby, I'm here now." Tatum sat on the bed and reached for Franklin's hand. Franklin turned his head, the cannula of the oxygen off of his nose. Tatum reached to fix it, but he shook his head.

"Tate? Baby girl?" he wheezed. "Baby girl, I know I'm late."

Tatum was confused. "Late? No Franklin, you're home. Not late."

"No. The restaurant. I'm late. Sorry."

It took a few minutes, but it dawned on Tatum that Franklin thought he was on their first date, where he'd been late. He had gotten a flat tire, and she had to wait for an hour. This was pre-cell phones and texts. Because she liked him, Tatum had waited for him. He arrived sweaty, grease-stained, and holding flowers. They ordered nachos and margaritas, and she fell head over heels for him. They had been inseparable ever since. Yet, tonight, she hadn't been there when he needed her most.

"It's ok, Frankie. I waited."

"Good." He smiled, holding on to her hand. His breathing slowed and his eyes closed. After a few minutes, he opened his eyes, returning his attention back to her. "Did you have fun, Tate?"

Tatum sniffed, wiping her eyes. "Fun?"

"Tonight. Secrets. Fun?"

"I…" Tatum paused. "It was fun,' she lied. She couldn't tell him about the shit that had happened tonight. Not now. It didn't matter.

"Good, beautiful. Good." His grip on her fingers loosened.

"Frankie?" Tears filled Tatum's eyes and dropped on the trench coat that she still wore.

His breathing slowed down to a slow wheeze as
Franklin closed his eyes. The monitors beeped, then
suddenly flatline as Franklin's body grew still. Zora
rushed in, but Tatum held up her hand to stop her.

"The funeral home's number is on my desk."

4

AN OATH

A cold plate of fried chicken, mac and cheese, and greens sat in front of Tatum, untouched.

"Ma, are you going to eat anything?" Morgan stroked his mother's shoulder as he sat next to her at the dining room table. "You haven't had a bite since last night."

Tatum watched as the thin sheen of grease coagulated across the crispy coating. It turned her stomach as she pushed the plate away. "No, baby. I just can't right now. Why don't you and Raheem go back to the campus. Lisa and I can finish cleaning up. I'll be fine."

Morgan held on to his boyfriend Raheem's hand and nodded. "Okay. But if you need anything, call me. I mean it. Any time." He bent down and kissed his mother on the temple, his short locs tickling the top of her nose. Tatum looked up into his face, a face that was near identical to his late father, except Morgan sported a full goatee. He was practically a grown man, so sure of himself at a young age. Just like his father. Tatum's heart ached at the thought of the things Franklin would miss out on like, Morgan's wedding, his first adult job, or grand-children.

"I'll come too Doc," said Raheem, her former T.A. whom Morgan had fallen madly for. She was so grateful that Morgan had Raheem to go through this with. Who did she have? Alisa couldn't dry her tears or kiss her and make it better. The one person who'd always eased that type of pain was gone, his loss being the reason for Tatum's current agony.

Tatum patted Raheem's hand and shooed him away with a smile, along with Morgan. "Ya'll take as much food as you want in those Tupperware containers. Share some of that cake with your friends."

When the last of the mourners had left, Tatum got up from the dining room table and tossed the plate of food in the trash. She reached in the fridge for the cold bottle of Grey Goose and poured herself a glass. She hated vodka, but honestly, it wasn't about the taste. She needed something to ease the pain and the guilt she felt. She shouldn't have gone to Secrets that night. She should have stayed and held Franklin's hand the entire time he suffered, not just for the last few minutes.

As Tatum was pouring another glass, Alisa rounded the corner. "Whoa, girl! I know you don't drink vodka, so what the hell are you doing?"

"Trying not to feel anything anymore."

Alisa eased the bottle and rocks glass out of Tatum's hands and guided her around to the barstools, encouraging her to sit. As soon as she did, Tatum sobbed into her hands.

"I was only there for his final breath. I shouldn't have listened to him. I should have stayed."

"But you were there! That matters, T."

Tatum sniffed, rubbing her runny nose against the sleeve of her wrap dress. "If I hadn't had seen Cassidy that night, God knows what I would have done."

"True! That reminds me! So, that night, I was getting my freak on with two cuties I met…"

Tatum tucked her lips into her mouth, trying her best not to remember the sight of her cousin sucking dick.

"Anyway," Alisa continued cautiously, aware of her cousin's reaction. "Just as I was about to cum for like the fifth time, who do I see but Cassidy, draped in a towel, approaching me. I thought to myself, 'This is my lucky night! It's about to go down.' He told me you went home, and when I was ready, just come find him."

Tatum raised a brow. "And where was he when you were ready to go?"

"Fully dressed and sitting at the bar by the dance floor."

For some strange reason, a wave of relief hit Tatum knowing Cassidy wasn't there fucking. She wasn't sure why.

"But that wasn't the craziest part. I'm thinking I'mma at least feel the dick in the car. Suck it. Something! He didn't say but a few words to me and just dropped me off at home. Nothing. Just said bye and peeled off! I barely had on any clothes, and you don't wanna fuck, and we just left a sex club? What a weirdo!"

Maybe because it wasn't you he wanted to fuck, thought Tatum. But she didn't dare say that out loud. "Maybe he'd gotten his fill at the club."

Alisa squinted her eyes at Tatum. "Did he say something to you to make you leave? Did he try to fuck you? Oh my god, did y'all actually fuck?"

"God, no! I just… I just couldn't go through with it. I had a panic attack and left and ran into him. Total shocker to me. Just glad he was there to look out for you." Tatum hoped that her lie was believable. Usually, Alisa was good at picking up when her cousin wasn't truthful. By the look on her face, Alisa wasn't sure if she fully believed Tatum. This time, she left it alone.

"Whatever. The man ain't look out for me, but I appreciated the ride home. It just wasn't the ride I wanted."

Both women chuckled softly until the laughter died down. Alisa took Tatum's hand and squeezed. "The service was beautiful. You sent Franklin home with the Lord in style."

"Funny thing is, he wasn't all that religious, but for his funeral, he definitely wanted a full Baptist service."

"Funerals are for the living," reminded Alisa. "Despite his own reservations about church, Frankie knew you all would need the comfort. He just wanted you to feel happy and not think about the pain he was in."

"But what about my pain, Alisa? It's never going to go away. I'll never be happy."

Alisa encircled her cousin in her arms, the full weight of her bosom cradling her head. She stroked Tatum, ignoring the fresh blow out she'd worked hard on hours before. "Stop that. You will. And the pain will always be there. Time doesn't lessen it, just gives you the tools to live with it."

Tatum said nothing as Alisa continued to rock her and stroke her hair. She felt like she was in the arms of her own mother, or even Alisa's mother, her aunt. She didn't want her to let go.

A gentle tapping noise interrupted their mutual consoling. The women both looked toward the noise to find Miles standing there, his head nearly touching the top of the door frame. He moved toward them at the kitchen island.

"Hey, ladies. Hey T, how you holding up?" He placed a gentle hand on Tatum's shoulder.

Tatum shook her head. "I don't know, Miles. I don't."

Miles shoved his hands in his pockets and rocked on his heels. "Listen, can I talk to you about something? In private? It's about Franklin."

Tatum's eyes grew wide as she looked at Alisa, who nodded. "Yeah. That's fine. Alisa, can you finish trying to find a place in the fridge for all this food? Just toss the stuff you know I will not eat. Or pack it up to take over to Aunt Dinah and Uncle Harold's place since they are homebound."

"Sure thing. Y'all go handle business. I'll be right here when you get back," assured Alisa as she began pulling out the aluminum foil and plastic wrap.

Miles put his hand on the small of Tatum's back, easing her out of the kitchen. "Let's go to your study, ok?"

Tatum nodded. She figured that this must be serious if he wanted to talk in the study. Was the firm in trouble financially? Did he want to talk about dividing up assets now? She didn't want to think about all the business crap just hours after she put Franklin in the ground. She thought Miles was a much more sensitive guy than that.

But when she got to her study, she found Deacon and Cassidy sitting on her leather sofa. She furrowed her brows, confused. What the hell did the three of them want to talk to her about? She thought of every scenario. Did Franklin owe money? Did he cheat and produce a child? God, had he been unfaithful throughout the entire marriage? The thought made Tatum nearly faint, but Miles held her steady.

"T? You okay? Please, sit down here." He pulled out the plush velvet chair in front of her desk for her to sit as he sat on the arm of the sofa.

"Miles, what is this about? Is the firm okay? Did Franklin do something?"

"No, T. The firm is fine. It's all good. Actually, this may be our best year in existence. Still hard without Franklin, though."

Miles looked over at Cassidy and Deacon, who both nodded. "Go on man," encouraged Deacon. "Tell her."

Miles ran a hand over his bald head as he began. "Tatum, you know Franklin was like a brother to us. I mean, Deacon and I have known him since law school back in Raleigh. And Cassidy—well, we picked him up along the way, but we've all been boys for a long time."

Tatum nodded with a knowing smile. "He loved you all like brothers too."

"The thing is, when Franklin told us he had lung cancer and had just a few months to live, he made us promise something to him. Several things, actually."

"Promise what?"

"To take care of you," interrupted Deacon, as he scratched the fluff of graying curls on his head. "If you ever needed anything, you were to call us first. Doesn't matter what it's about. The house. Money. Morgan. Anything."

Tatum smiled. "That is very sweet, Deek. And I know you guys are so kind and will look out for me. But I don't need money. Franklin took care of that. And I don't need..."

"That's not what we mean," Cassidy interrupted. He chewed on his bottom lip. "I mean, yeah, all of that too, but Franklin wanted us to be…there for you. In any capacity."

Tatum's brows knit in confusion, his emphasis on the word *any* not making things clearer. "And like I said…you don't have to be. I'm well taken care of."

The trio looked at each other, frustrated. Tatum wasn't here for this cryptic game. "Listen, is there something you all aren't telling me? I feel you're talking in riddles. And right now, hours after burying my husband, that's something I can't deal with."

"Fuck it," said Cassidy. "Tatum, the reason I was at Secrets that night is that Franklin told us what he asked you to do. And I had to make sure you didn't go through with it."

Tatum's eyes were wide with horror. She felt heat rush to her face. "Why? Why would he tell you that? That was our business—*my* business! Are you trying to embarrass me?" She was actually a little disappointed that this conversation would not be about a mistress or a break baby.

Cassidy shook his head, apologetically. "No, Tatum, not at all. It's just…we told him that was a dumb thing to ask. You're already under so much stress and we know you'd never say no to Frankie. Plus, just months before, he'd asked one of us to take care of those needs for you."

Tatum's eyes bulged at what she heard. "Say what?"

Deacon sighed. "He wanted us to handle the sex stuff for him. Because he couldn't anymore and you seemed so sad and lonely. We were like, 'Hell no. We not doing this.' But he said he would rather the next man you sleep with be familiar and not a stranger. But we said nah, so I guess he concocted this Secrets plan."

Tatum sat back in the chair. "Frankie…he can't…I mean… He shouldn't have done that. I am not his property to will to the next man. This isn't ancient times. "

"I know," said Miles. "And I agree. You can do whatever you want. But Tatum, Secrets? I know you were honoring Frankie's wishes, but baby girl, you don't need that place."

"Why? Because I have you all?"

"Yes," Miles said matter-of-factly.

"And you were there the whole time?" Tatum directed her question at Cassidy, whose face turned redder by the second. His full beard couldn't hide it.

"I was. I saw you and Alisa come in, and I just watched you. And when that guy, that toddler who'd been eyeing you the minute you walked in, approached you, I knew I had to step in."

"You didn't have to yank me into a dark-ass room

and threaten me! You scared the shit out of me, Cass! I thought someone was trying to assault me. God!"

"Good lord," mumbled Miles.

"You threatened her?" asked Deacon. "Damn, Cass, you need to get a hold of your anger issues."

"It wasn't a threat, Deacon. I was just trying to look out for her."

Cassidy turned his attention toward Tatum. "I just wanted to get you out of there. Get you to go home. I am so sorry if you felt that way. I never meant to scare you. I'd seen that young cat fuck a few chicks before you, and that youngster wouldn't be satisfied until he had you. I was just trying to look out for you. That's all."

So, explain the boner, Tatum thought. But she didn't want, or need, to bring that up. "So, what now? What are you asking me to do? To choose between the three of you? Who gets to fuck Frankie's widow next? He isn't even cold in the ground yet!"

Tatum instantly regretted sounding so harsh, but she was angry and confused. What the fuck was going on? Why had Frankie asked his best friends to do this? Never once had he treated her like a piece of ass to be pawned off to any man. Clearly, the cancer had inhibited his ability to make sane decisions. "Listen, y'all. Franklin is gone. You don't have to go through with this ridiculous plan to take care of me." Tatum did air quotes around *take care of.* "I have other shit to focus on. Like going back to teaching. And Morgan needs me."

"Morgan is a grown ass man, T," laughed Deacon. "He's not a baby anymore. He's doing his thing and killing it. Shit, Mo got a man now and everything. I mean, he'll always need his mom, but...you have needs too."

Tatum folded her arms. "What do you know about my needs?"

"I saw the look in your eyes that night, Tatum. When that boy touched you, your body reacted. You have needs, Mama," said Cassidy.

Tatum swallowed, instinctively squeezed her thighs together at the way Cassidy said "mama." It damn sure wasn't the way Morgan said it. The men's eyes followed her every movement. Dear God. It felt like she was under some sexual inquisition with Miles, Deacon, and Cassidy as her judges, jury, and executioners, trying to decide which one of them was going to put her out of her misery first.

"Miles, you just got divorced!"

Miles rolled his eyes. "It's been three years, Tatum. And there's been no one serious since Paula. I don't get around like that."

She pointed. "But Deacon! You'll fuck anything in sight!"

Deacon let out a low chuckle. "That's true. I do be having hoes, but I've always been safe. If you need an STI panel, I got you. But right now, my focus is on you, Tatum. Taking care of you means with or with nothing sexual." Deacon's eyes flew to Miles, who simply smirked.

Tatum turned her attention toward Cassidy, who seemed to brace himself for whatever she had to say to him. "And Cassidy... I... I just don't know you well enough to consent to anything," was all that she could come up with.

Cassidy smirked, the glint of a gold grill visible. "I think you know me, Tatum. I think you know me well enough."

At that moment, Tatum knew he knew that she'd seen that massive dick poking behind that towel at Secrets. She cleared her throat. "If you say so."

All three men looked at each other before Miles spoke. "Listen, we aren't asking you to make a choice right now. Or even to choose. I know the whole scenario is wild as hell. But just know we're here for you. Okay? This isn't just about sex, T. It's about whatever you need."

"Whatever," repeated Deacon, not a hint of his usual sarcasm in his voice.

Tatum scoffed. "How do I know that? For all I know, you all could be making this whole thing up."

Miles nodded. "He thought you'd say that." With that, Miles pulled out his phone and pulled up a voice note. "Play it."

Tatum reached for the phone and pressed play. At first, she heard the familiar sound of whirring and beeps of Franklin's machines, and then Franklin's voice.

"Hey, beautiful. If you're listening to this, then I'm gone and Miles is playing this message for you. I know, a little strange to hear my voice after I'm gone. It's going to be really hard without me. But Miles, Deek, and Cass are there for you. Lean on them when you get sad, lonely, want to cry, or, hell, want to laugh. Want a date to dinner? Call them. When you need to feel muscular arms around you or something more, call on them. People are going to pressure you to get back out there, but I know you. You don't need strangers, you need the familiar. With that, I give you permission to be happy. I believe one of these three jokers is the right man for the job. I trust them. They promised me they would do right by you. To fulfill your every need and fantasy for you. On my behalf. Bye, Tate. I love you. Forever and always."

Tears rolled down Tatum's face as she handed Miles back his phone.

"Just think about it. In whatever capacity you

choose, we are going to honor Frankie's wishes." Miles motioned for the fellas to get up and leave. They all rose and headed for the door. Tatum remained seated as Miles placed a gentle hand on Tatum's shoulder and squeezed. Deacon kissed her gently on the cheek. But Cassidy lingered behind.

"I'm sorry I scared you," he repeated.

"It's fine."

He crouched down at her side. "It's not fine, Tatum. I have a temper sometimes. They are right. I gotta handle that shit."

Tatum watched as Cassidy's eyes followed the curve of her legs, her wrap dress showing a little more thigh than she wanted to. Alisa was right. All of Frankie's friends were fine. But Cassidy Valentine was mysterious and brooding. Even his name was sexy. That combination made him especially dangerous.

Tatum shook her head. Nope. She shouldn't be thinking about that at a time like this. "I accept your apology. Now, can you go?"

Cassidy rose from his knee. He got to the door and turned to her. "Think about it, Tatum." And with that, he left.

Tatum sat paralyzed in her study, her body unable to rise from its seat until she heard the front door close. They must be crazy to think that she'd consider something like sleeping with one of them. Or asking any of them for anything. Franklin clearly should have talked to her about this. She knew that if he did, she would have talked him out of this wild plan and probably talked to the doctor about such a delusion.

In a stupor, Tatum walked back into the kitchen to find Alisa wrapping up a plate of deviled eggs while munching on one. Tatum said nothing and sat at the breakfast nook, staring out the bay window behind her.

"Are you alright? What was this meeting of the three amigos about?" Alisa put the last of the Tupperware she was taking with her in a bag and joined Tatum at the table.

Tatum turned her head, slowly. "It was…something to do with Frankie's will." She lied. There was absolutely no way she could tell her cousin that Frankie's three best friends had taken an oath to take care of her, which included fucking her out of her misery.

"I know them dudes ain't talking to you about no money or things! Frankie ain't even cold!"

"I can't talk about it right now. Today has been a lot."

Alisa backed away. "Um, okay. You sure you're okay?"

"I'm good."

"Want me to make you some coffee?"

Tatum shook her head. "No. I'll take some of Aunt Bertie's sweet potato pie and a bourbon on the rocks. Frankie hid some behind the old cookie tin, thinking that I wouldn't find it."

Alisa squeezed her cousin's hand. "Sure thing, babe. I got you."

5

COMMITTED TO MEMORY

*C*lass, make sure you have your essays to me by midnight on Friday. Next week, we dig into Walker's examination of the failures of masculinity in *The Color Purple*. Read the book! Don't watch the movie."

As Tatum's senior seminar students filed out of the classroom, she blew out a breath. She'd made it through her first week back at the university. Aside from her colleagues asking how she was doing every five minutes, and the occasional, annoying student who was attempting to be a kiss-ass so early in the semester, Tatum had made it out fairly unscathed. She'd only cried in her office a few times during the week, nearly certain her T.A. had heard her but hadn't pried.

She was grateful that she'd come back to work

53

during the summer semester versus fall, when it was absolutely chaotic. She could ease back into the groove of academia with an abbreviated schedule and without all the other bullshit obligations that came with being the chair of the English department.

Tatum walked across campus to her office in Grover Hall. Luckily, the walk was short, and the heat hadn't destroyed her wash-and-go. She was grateful for the gust of air conditioning that she felt as soon as she opened the doors to the building, but unease quickly replaced her smile as she walked down the hall toward her office. Standing outside her door was a young man, tall and honey-brown, leaning against the wall. The closer Tatum got, the more familiar the face of the young man became. When Tatum was within two feet, her unease was replaced with horror and dread as she realized why the face was so familiar.

Tatum cleared her throat, pushing up her glasses. "Can I help you, young man?" Her eyes scanned the young man's face, then flitted across his chest as the familiar imprint of his nipple rings was visible through his t-shirt.

The young man looked up from his phone and smiled. "Hi. Dr. Simmons? I am Jason. Jason Duggar. I wanted to come by because I missed your senior seminar class this morning. I was in financial aid getting stuff sorted out with my scholarship."

Tatum nodded, pressing her portfolio against her chest. She felt as if her heart was thumping against it, trying to break free. "That's fine. You could have emailed. No need for you to come by. I'll send you the syllabus." As she turned to open her office, Jason leaned closer.

"Dr. Simmons, my mother raised me better than that. I thought it the proper thing to do to come in person and introduce myself. This is my last year here, and I don't wanna screw it up. My parents would kill me."

Tatum looked up at the young man and squinted, scanning for a sign that he recognized her. When he backed away, a little embarrassed, Tatum realized maybe he didn't recognize her at all. She was instantly relieved.

"Well, Mr. Duggar, I appreciate the respect and I am glad you came by in person. I'll email you the syllabus, and I expect you to catch up with the first week's reading." She paused and looked at him as he nodded. "Just curious, but have you taken any of my classes before?" Tatum was clearly pulling at straws.

Jason frowned, confused. "Uh. No, ma'am. I'm an English minor and pre-med. I'm a little behind on my minor credits because of my year in Senegal. My parents do medical missions there. I celebrated my twenty-first birthday there. Kinda cool."

Tatum covered her mouth, nearly screaming in horror. A twenty-one-year-old boy was trying to fuck her brains out months ago in a sex club. Thank God she didn't go through with it. And thank God for Cassidy.

"Something wrong, Dr. Simmons?" asked Jason, curious why Tatum had gone stone-stiff.

"Nothing. I…I just remembered I have a meeting, so if you'll excuse me."

Tatum quickly opened her office door and slammed it closed before she could hear another word from Jason's mouth. She cursed herself.

Dammit, Frankie! You had me damn nearly fucking one of my students. Tatum rubbed her temples as she sat at her desk. She'd dodged a bullet, thanks to Cassidy.

Cassidy.

Tatum hadn't talked to Cassidy, Miles, or Deacon since the night of Franklin's funeral. She'd dodged every text and phone call. What could she say to them? It seemed absolutely preposterous to even entertain such an arrangement. How the hell would that even work? After being with one man for twenty-two years, how could she possibly think about trying to be with someone else?

Tatum opened her laptop and answered some emails. Most were from colleagues checking on her, and some were from conferences with calls for papers. She paused at one from Dawson and Simmons, Attorneys at Law, dated three hours ago.

From: Dawson@DawsonandSimmons.com
To: Tatum.Simmons@DecaturState.com
Subject: Call Me, or….

Tate,

If I don't hear from you by lunch, I'm coming to your office.

Miles Dawson
Founding Partner
Dawson and Simmons, Attorneys at Law

Tatum rolled her eyes. Yeah, right. With Franklin gone, Miles was far too busy to take time from his busy schedule to hunt her down at her office. The man was a workaholic to a fault. No sooner than she had the thought, she heard a knock at her door.

"Tate, open the door. I know you're there. I can smell your perfume in the hallway."

Tatum peered over her laptop screen and saw the

shadow of a lanky figure at her door. It was Miles, just as he'd promised.

"Come in, Miles."

Miles slowly opened the door, revealing his nearly 6'5" frame, well-dressed in a gray suit with a gray, navy, and white-striped tie. Since the last time they'd seen each other, he'd grown a low, neatly trimmed beard. He looked good. Fantastic.

"Guess I need to stop wearing Tom Ford," she mumbled.

Miles pulled out a seat in front of her desk and crossed his long legs, his foot resting on his knee. "I said I'd be here if you didn't answer me."

"What is it, Miles? I had a seminar class, or did you forget that I actually taught classes?"

Miles smiled as he adjusted his cufflinks. "I'm aware. It's also lunchtime. You have to eat. Let me take you to lunch. We can talk."

Tatum folded her arms. "Miles, in the nearly twenty-something years I've known you, you hardly ever take lunch. Don't you have work to do?"

"I've cleared my calendar for a few hours."

Tatum sighed. "Miles, I have nothing to say."

"Then we go to lunch and say nothing. What do you have a taste for?

Clearly, Miles wasn't letting up. Tatum grabbed her purse with attitude and stood. "You're buying me the dirtiest martini and the most expensive lobster."

Miles smirked as he rose from his chair. "Whatever the lady wants."

They sat at a booth in the back of Atlanta Fish Market, deep in a staring contest for the past thirty minutes. Tatum watched Miles over the rim of her glass as she sipped her martini slowly. The consummate neat freak, he'd carefully removed his suit jacket, put his cufflinks in his pocket, and rolled up his sleeves before cutting into his steak, medium-rare, like he liked it. Miles chewed slowly as he stared at Tatum staring at him.

"So, are we going to talk or just gape like children?" Miles asked as he dabbed the corners of his mouth with a napkin.

"I haven't decided yet."

Tatum dipped a piece of her lobster thermidor in drawn butter before placing it in her mouth. She chewed slowly, so slowly as to annoy Miles. This, however, only made him smile as he pushed his glasses back.

"You've always been so stubborn, Tate. It was the thing Frankie loved about you. "

"Don't bring Frankie up," reprimanded Tatum. "Don't."

"Why not?"

"Because it's still too raw."

"It's always going to be raw, Tate. For a while at least."

"Besides, you're being too damn empathetic for a guy who's trying to fuck his best friend's widow."

Miles took a sip of his McCallen and leaned back. "That's what you think this is about? Sex?"

"What else is this about? Clearly, Frankie thought he could just pawn me off to his boys so they can get a piece or something."

"Did you listen to any of what Frankie said? It's about making sure we met all of your needs. Done with respect and care, from people who already love you. We care about your happiness."

"You can do all that without sleeping with me."

"It can be whatever arrangement you'd like. Financial. Sexual. Emotional. Whatever makes you feel comfortable."

"What if I say no?"

"Then you say no. But I'd feel pretty shitty breaking an oath to Frankie, even in death. Wouldn't you?"

Tatum thought about all the promises she'd made to Franklin over the years, not breaking any of them.

This included the one where she'd ended up at Secrets. Keeping that promise could have resulted in something detrimental, like sleeping with her twenty-one-year-old student.

"And what are Deacon and Cassidy saying about all this?"

"They are on board with whatever you want as well. We aren't moving forward without your consent and a discussion between the four of us. You're running this."

"This is crazy, you know that, right? Tatum picked up an asparagus spear and bit into it, annoyed.

Miles chuckled. "Frankie was a crazy dude. We both know this. But he was also a man who never did a thing without thinking it through. I think he had his reasons for asking us to consider this arrangement."

"Like what?"

"Trust, maybe? He knew he could trust us without a doubt. Maybe he knew we'd never hurt you. We could never sit back and watch you get hurt by some dude. Not when we're here."

Tatum took a long sip of her martini, then sighed. "I trust you all as well. But right now, I can't even consider it. Give me some time."

Miles nodded. "Take as long as you need."

Despite her initial hesitancy, lunch with Miles took a pleasant turn. They reminisced about old times, telling stories about Frankie that made them laugh until their eyes watered and their sides hurt. Tatum enjoyed laughing for the first time in a while. It was the first time she could talk about Franklin without breaking down. It was also the first time she'd gone out with a man who wasn't Frankie or a colleague in nearly twenty years. It was different.

After another round of drinks, they called it an afternoon and Miles brought Tatum back to campus for her evening classes. Grover Hall was quiet, their steps against the linoleum echoing off the walls.

When they got to her door, Tatum turned to Miles. "Lunch turned out to be nice. Guess I needed that."

Miles gave her a warm smile. "Good."

"Cool. I'll be in touch." Tatum opened her arms, welcoming Miles in for a hug. Miles bent down, his large hands firmly on her back. Tatum felt him inhale, his hands slowly moving down her back to her hips as he pulled her in closer. Involuntarily, she relaxed into his grip and froze when his lips grazed the shell of her ear, the heat of his breath warming the curve of her neck.

"In twenty years, I've committed your scent to memory, Tatum. You can't change it. I won't let you."

A shiver went down Tatum's spine as she pulled away from Miles' embrace.

"I…I've got a class to teach."

In her office, Tatum rested her back against the wall next to the door. Her breathing felt erratic. For the second time that day, Tatum closed the door on a man who'd made her think and feel things she shouldn't.

Tatum looked up at the ceiling and blew out a breath.

It was going to be a long summer.

6

THUNDERSTORMS

The rain beat hard against Tatum's bedroom window. The boom of the thunder and crackle of the lightning had kept her awake most of the night. She hated summer thunderstorms. She looked over at her empty bed, rubbing the cool emptiness. If Franklin were there, he'd wrap his long legs around her, his locs grazing her arms as he embraced her.

"Don't worry, beautiful. We gotta have a little rain if we want the flowers," he'd always say.

Tatum thought about calling Morgan, but changed her mind when she looked at the time on her phone. It was nearly 3 a.m. and he would be up soon, starting the day at his summer internship in D.C. He'd need all the rest he could get working on Capitol Hill. Tears filled Tatum's eyes as she thought

64

about her son all grown up. When Morgan was little, a thunderstorm like this would have him begging Tatum and Franklin if he could sleep between the two of them. They'd never deny his request. He'd snuggle between them with his teddy bear and fall fast asleep.

But those years with Franklin and Morgan were now gone. She was alone for the first time in years. Terrifying was too small a word for how she felt.

Tatum turned on the lamp on her nightstand and reached for the remote. After a few times scrolling through the channels, she couldn't find anything to watch that interested her. She looked at her phone and, without thinking, decided to FaceTime the one person who she thought could be up.

"Tatum?" Miles answered her on the first ring. Tatum could see his face, glasses still perched on his nose. "Is everything okay?"

"Yeah. Well, no. I couldn't sleep. And then I remembered, you always worked late into the night. I took a chance to see if you were still up."

Miles chuckled softly. "Yeah, you know how I do. Of course, I'm up. Hold on." He repositioned the phone on his desk. Tatum could see more of him. He was shirtless, his lean, muscular chest prominent on the screen. Tatum's eyes followed the happy trail of hair leading down his stomach. She wondered if he had on boxers or briefs, or if he was clothed at all. "I can see you a lot better this way. So, why can't you sleep?"

Tatum positioned her phone on the stand near her lamp, propping herself on her side. "I hate storms like this. Always have." Just as she said that, a crack of lightning shot blue across her window, making Tatum squeal. "Sorry. Storms make me jumpy. I'm not used to being alone like this during one."

"I'm sure. You can talk to me for as long as you'd like. I'm just up preparing for a case."

"Oh? What case?"

"Remember that young man that Cobb County police pulled over for a busted taillight and claimed he reached for their gun? I am representing the family in a wrongful death suit."

Tatum nodded. "I remember that. So sad."

"Yeah. It's going to be a bitch. Just want to get my ducks all in a row."

Tatum nodded, but she knew Miles would do more than have his ducks in a row. He was meticulous to a fault. So much so that Frankie often complained that paralegals were a waste, because Miles was going to double, sometimes quadruple-check things.

"Well, get some rest. I won't disturb you."

Miles raised a brow. "Did I say you were disturbing me? "

"Why no, but…"

"I said you can talk to me as long as you want. So, talk about whatever you want until you get sleepy. I'm all ears."

Tatum smiled. "I appreciate that."

Miles leaned back in his chair. "How long have you been afraid of thunderstorms?"

"Pretty much all my life. Hell, I don't even like to drive in them. I'll pull over on the side of the road and wait it out."

"Why?"

Tatum let out a breath. "It was a thunderstorm that killed my parents. My dad was a pastor. They were coming home from a revival. The visibility on the road back from Augusta was low because of the rain, but they wanted to get home. The first day of school was the next day, and they'd never miss it. But…they died in a head-on collision with a tractor trailer who'd crossed the median of the highway."

"Gosh, Tate. I knew you lost your parents young, but I did not know it was that awful. I am sorry to hear that."

"It's fine. That was ages ago. I was like…11, almost 12. I had to go live with my grandma in Waycross after that. So…"

There was a growing silence between them, but Tatum looked into Miles' eyes. They were sympathetic yet deep, soulful brown eyes that sparkled behind his glasses. Tatum hadn't noticed that before. A loud boom shook the windows, and Tatum pulled the covers up to her neck.

"What would Franklin do when it stormed?"

Tatum smiled. "He'd wrap his legs around me and hold me." She giggled as she thought about Franklin's dick usually poking her in the ass and one thing leading to another.

"What's so funny?" Miles asked with a smile.

"Nothing. Just thinking about how… I guess thunderstorms make Frankie a little horny. Sorry. That's TMI."

Miles smirked, licking the corner of his lips. "I see. They do that for me sometimes too."

That involuntary action of Miles' tongue made Tatum's mind as electrically charged as an actual rain cloud.

"If I was there, I'd hold you," said Miles. "If I didn't live across town, I'd be there. No question. I think I'm tall enough to wrap my legs around you."

"No. I couldn't have you drive in this rain."

"I would, though."

Tatum repositioned herself onto her elbows, the

strap of her nightgown lazily falling down her shoulder. "Just to hold me?

"Hold you. Touch you," Miles pointed to the camera. "Kiss that bare shoulder right there…whatever."

Even with just the bare shoulders, suddenly Tatum felt naked. "Oh."

"What are you wearing under that duvet?" Miles pushed his glasses up, moving closer to the phone.

"Just a nightgown."

"Can I see it?"

Tatum bit her lip, unsure if she should do this. But it was late. And she was alone. Lonely. She slid the heavy down duvet toward her feet, exposing her plain, black silk nightgown. Her breast spilled out of the top slightly, and Tatum moved to cover herself.

"Don't," said Miles. "I want to see you. All of you."

Tatum moved her hands. She'd never been this self-conscious of her body, but now, in this moment, Miles staring at her made her feel raw. Exposed.

"You're beautiful, Tate. Your breasts, your skin. Everything." Miles was staring at her as if he were seeing her with fresh eyes. Minus a swimsuit here or there when they used to vacation as a group, Tatum was sure that he'd never seen her nearly naked. This entire experience was new.

"Even in a headscarf?" Tatum tried to deflect his

examination with laughter, but Miles' eyes remained focused. Tatum felt her breathing slow down and her skin, despite the coolness of her bedroom, on fire. "And…what are you wearing?"

Miles slowly stood up, revealing a visible erection in black boxer briefs. Jesus Christ! Tatum swallowed because she did not know Miles was that hung. The print was thicker than she imagined.

"Just boxers. You like them?"

Tatum nodded, unable to say anything else. Miles watched as her eyes lingered there. His hands followed, stroking his length outside of his boxers. Tatum let out the smallest of gasps, feeling her pussy tense at the sight of him.

"When's the last time you touched yourself, Tatum?" asked Miles, nearly verbatim to Frankie's inquiry weeks before.

"It's been a while," she confessed.

"I want you to do that. But first, sit up."

Tatum did as she was told, her legs hanging off the bed.

"Take those straps down, show me those beautiful tits, baby girl."

Tatum closed her eyes and did that. The pulsation between her legs was becoming stronger, like a honing beacon, directing Miles to the center of her desire. Tatum watched as Miles sat back down, his chair pushed back far enough to where she could see him continuing to stroke himself, this time his hands clearly inside his boxers.

"Look at those pretty, round nipples. Those deep chocolate areolas. Like silver dollars. I wish I could take one in my mouth. Hmm… Why don't you do that for me?"

Tatum's brow rose. "You want me to…"

Miles nodded. "Suck your nipple. Suck it as if I were there."

Tatum lifted one breast, bending down slightly, and allowing her tongue to circle her nipple. Within seconds, it was hard against her tongue. She sucked, flicking her tongue across both her nipples and around her deep cocoa-colored areolas. An electric sensation coursed through her body as she slipped her hand between her thighs, stroking her already-sensitive clit.

"Tell me what you're doing," Miles asked between ragged breaths as he stroked his dick, now visible, its head shiny and coated with a generous amount of precum. "Tell me."

"I'm touching my pussy."

"Good, baby girl. Push two fingers inside. I want to hear how wet you are."

Tatum did as she was told. Her folds were slick, hot, and wet. The noises her wet pussy made seemed to drown out any of the rain that beat against her window. She couldn't remember the last time she was this aroused. It seemed like ages ago. Tatum pressed two fingers, then three, inside herself, using her thumb to circle her clit. She was so close to coming, but she didn't want to. She wanted to hold on to this feeling for a while. Who knew when she'd feel it again.

"Look at that pretty-ass face. You want to come, don't you, Tate?"

"Yes," Tatum breathed, her chest heaving. It had been ages since she masturbated, and she wasn't sure how long she was going to last.

"Should I let you come?" asked Miles as he spit into his hand and continued stroking.

Tatum was so turned on that she was dizzy. She threw her head back and moaned.

"Yes. Miles, let me come. Please?"

"Not yet." Miles gave Tatum a sexy smirk. "Stroke faster, love. Harder."

Tatum groaned, feeling her abdomen tighten as her fingers were coated with her creamy wetness. "Ugh, Miles... I—" But before Tatum could finish that sentence, she felt her pussy tighten around her fingers and she came. Her moans echoed off the walls as her body shivered in delight.

"You naughty girl. I told you not to come yet, didn't I?"

Tatum looked at Miles, whose face was contorted with pleasure. He was close too. His chest seemed to glisten with a light sheen of sweat as he pumped into his hand.

"Tate, I'm so close."

After a minute, Miles grunted as cum shot onto his stomach and chest in thick streams. Tatum wanted to lick it off, slurping and savoring the taste. Tatum wondered how Miles would feel inside her pussy. In her mouth. In her ass.

"Next time, I'm coming in that pretty mouth of yours," said Miles, as if he'd read her mind. He reached for a Kleenex on his desk and gently wiped his chest and abdomen.

The thought made her nipples, still exposed in the cool air, tighten again. She hadn't had dirty thoughts about a man other than Franklin in over twenty years. She certainly hadn't ever had phone sex with anyone besides him. She felt both aroused and ashamed.

"Seriously, how do you feel?" asked Miles as he continued to clean himself.

Relaxed. Blissful. Tatum wanted to say that. Instead, she simply replied, "I'm good."

"Good." Miles tossed the tissue into a wastebasket next to the desk and gently adjusted his glasses.

"You didn't take your glasses off," observed Tatum as she watched his post-orgasmic ritual. "Do you keep them on during sex?"

Miles laughed. "Normally I wouldn't. Would you like me to next time?"

Tatum frowned playfully. "Who said there was going to be a next time?"

"There's going to be next time. Possibly with our clothes off. In person. But I'd at least like to take you to dinner first. I am a gentleman, after all."

"What makes you so sure?"

Miles adjust the waistband of his shorts. "Because phone sex isn't enough for a woman like you."

"A woman like me? What's that? Old? Lonely?"

Miles frowned. "Don't talk down about yourself, Tate. You're forty-four, not ancient. And you're not alone. You have me. And the fellas," He picked up the phone, his face now closer to the screen. "I mean a woman who has a body that needs to be touched. Held. A grown woman with needs."

Tatum's face felt hot. "Oh." Tatum looked at the time on her phone. "It's damn near four and you'll need to be at work soon."

"Did you forget that I'm the boss? I can go in when I want."

Tatum laughed awkwardly as she pulled up the straps of her nightgown. "Right." She didn't know how to get off the phone now. She felt like a silly teenager who'd just said her first dirty words to a boy.

Sensing her unease, Miles took the lead. "Why don't you get some sleep? I think the rain has eased up now."

"I will. Goodnight."

"I promise, next time I'll come over. I don't care how bad it's raining."

Tatum smiled. "Okay."

"And Tatum? Stop overthinking things."

"What do you mean?"

"We just had a little of fun. Don't feel guilty about it. I know how your mind works."

He was right, as usual. Tatum nodded. "Right. Goodnight, Miles."

Tatum laid back on her pillow, falling asleep within minutes, satisfied for the first time in ages.

7

GIRLS' NIGHT

*T*atum tried her best to keep focused on the departmental meeting. As department chair, discussions regarding the budget for the next academic year were on the agenda and very important. Yet, the boring nature of the entire conversation was making her doze off. It also hadn't helped that she'd been up till four in the morning having phone sex with one of her dead husband's best friends.

Once the discussion concluded, Tatum thought it best that they table the rest of the conversation regarding accreditation. She didn't think she could handle anymore of Dr. Grover's monotone voice and Dr. Palametto's constant sniffing between sentences. On her way back to her office, she stopped by the mailboxes in the main office to see if she'd received anymore fellowship applications.

"Hey, Lydia. How are you doing?" asked Tatum as she stopped by the receptionist desk.

Lydia smiled. "I'm good, Dr. Tatum. So good to see you. This office has been dull as dishwater with you not around."

Tatum laughed. "I am sure Dr. Conway's Shakespeare-themed jokes were entertaining."

Lydia rolled her eyes. "Barely. By the way, you had a delivery come for you. I put it in your office."

"Thanks, Lydia."

After checking her mailbox, Tatum hurried down the hallway to her office. She opened her door and gasped. There was a massive bouquet of yellow daisies on her desk, and next to it, a gold box wrapped in red ribbon. Curious, Tatum examined the vase of flowers. There was no note. She sat at her desk and slid the box towards her. Slowly, she opened it, and a card fell out.

"So you won't run out."

Tatum lifted the smaller box inside, realizing it was a bottle of Tom Ford perfume.

Miles...

Tatum pulled out her phone and shot him a quick

text, thanking him for the flowers and perfume and insisting that he didn't have to send either.

MILES

I know. I wanted to.

TATUM

Thanks.

Just ask she was typing her text to Miles, her phone buzzed. It was a text from Deacon.

DEACON

So how long are you going to keep ignoring me like a $2 whore?

Tatum nearly choked out a laugh.

Tatum

I'm not ignoring you, Deacon. I am just…thinking.

DEACON

Does this mean you've decided?

TATUM

No, I'm sorry.

For a while, a few dots appeared and disappeared on the screen. Finally, Deacon replied.

DEACON

Is it because I am part of this
arrangement? I mean, I get it. I don't
think you've ever liked me, anyway.

Tatum's eyes widened as she replied.

TATUM

That's not true, Deek! And you know
it. I just always thought maybe one
day you'd grow up and maybe settle
down.

DEACON

As the kids say, heaux is life.

Tatum let out a laugh.

TATUM

Right. So, in this scenario, would I be
one of your heauxs?

DEACON

Never. You're too precious for that.

Tatum's heart squeezed a bit at Deacon's words.

TATUM

Thanks.

DEACON

Go on and teach, Doc. I'll holler at
you later.

Tatum put her phone away, turning her attention

to her schedule and lesson plans for her next seminar class. But then she thought. She'd heard from Miles and Deacon. No Cassidy. Nothing since their meeting after the funeral. Maybe he'd come to his senses and changed his mind about the entire thing. If so, that was fine with Tatum. She'd just wish that he'd communicate that with her.

Wait... Was she wanting to hear from him?

Tatum's mind wandered to that night at Secrets and how Cassidy's eyes bore into her. How his voice boomed and made her wet, and how his dick was at attention, even amid ordering her to leave.

That differed from Miles, whose voice the other night had been soft, seductive, and gently commanding. A wave of heat coursed over her body at the thought of how he'd guided her through masturbating and how she just wanted to please him. It seemed very reminiscent of Franklin.

Tatum ran a hand through her hair and scratched her scalp furiously, as if she was scratching away the thought of Cassidy and Miles. *What is wrong with me?* She couldn't think about either of them anymore. She had to get her mind off of the entire situation. She pulled out her phone again and dialed.

"Hey, Alisa, what are you doing tonight?"

"Girl, nothing. I got maybe two more heads to do before I call it a day." Tatum could hear the clack of hair curlers and loud salon conversations in the background.

"Want to go by and pay Nadine a visit? Bring over some food and kick it with her? Since she's on bedrest?"

Nadine had been Tatum and Alisa's childhood friend, having met when she was living next door to Tatum's grandmother in Waycross. Now, Nadine was pregnant with her second child from her second marriage. It was high risk, and she was on what seemed like perpetual bedrest.

"Oh! Let's do that. It's been a minute since we checked in on her."

"Cool. I'll tell Eddie that we are coming by. It'll be a surprise. She could use the company. I'll pick up some tacos."

"Sweet! I'll being the tequila... wait... Nadine can't drink. I'll bring grape juice for her."

Tatum laughed. "Okay. See you there around 6?"

"Bet!"

Tatum balanced a box full of tacos, salsa, chips and all the dips as she rang the doorbell a second time to Nadine's massive West Midtown mansion.

Alisa blew out a breath. "Man, I always forget

that Nadine is fucking loaded! It probably takes her forty minutes to get to the front door."

Tatum looked over at Alisa, who also balanced a few bags of wine, tequila, and juice. The two of them together looked like a walking UberEATS and a distillery.

"Well, I hope she isn't getting up. She should have Alex or Eddie come open the door."

As soon as she said those words, a bright eyed, afro-puff wearing girl opened the door. "Auntie Tate! Auntie Lisa! What are y'all doing here?"

Tatum leaned in for a kiss on the cheek. "Alex, we came to see your mom and surprise her with her favorite! Tacos!"

Alex blew out a breath. "Good, because she's getting on my nerves!" She ushered the women in, taking a bag out of Alisa's hand as she talked a mile a minute. "Mama is miserable that she's on bedrest, so she's ordering me to do the most minute things! Changing all the remote batteries! Checking the thermostat every ten minutes. And poor Eddie! She's running him ragged. I feel for the man."

Tatum laughed. "Baby girl, that's pregnancy for you."

The three of them headed to the kitchen, where they placed all the food and drinks on the massive island. Once their hands were free, they all exchanged hugs, with the women remarking on how tall and beautiful Alex was. Alex blushed.

"And how is Morgan?" Alex asked. Tatum knew Alex had the biggest crush on Morgan, even after she found out he was gay.

"He's still gay, Alex," Alisa quipped. Tatum busted out laughing as Alex frowned.

"Damn!" Alex snapped her fingers. "Oh well. Wait? Is that tequila? Can I have some?"

"Alex! You're not even eighteen yet!" scolded Tatum. "I will not be contributing to the delinquency of a minor."

"I'm seventeen. I'll be in college soon!"

"Alex, get your narrow behind out those bags! Let your mom know we are here," laughed Alisa.

"You heard what she said," said the weary voice of Nadine as she rounded the corner, shuffling her no doubt swollen feet in her slippers. "Get out of here, Alex!"

"Fine! But not without payment! Kid tax!" Alex huffed, snatching a few chips and guacamole as she left the kitchen.

The ladies chuckled as they embraced for a hug. Nadine was all belly in her maternity dress, but she looked amazing. Her bright, tawny complexion glowed, and her hair, pulled up in a messy top-knot, was shiny. She'd never looked more beautiful.

"Wow, you are carrying a lot honey!" remarked Alisa. "You sure that's just one baby?"

Nadine rolled her eyes. "Stop asking me dumb shit. You know it's just one baby. A big baby, but one baby. Eddie can finally chill now that he's getting a son!'

"A son!" squealed Tatum. "Oh, how wonderful!"

"Yeah, for Eddie!" snapped Nadine. "I'm used to dealing with girls. I am not looking forward to getting projectile peed on or being layered head to toe in sports attire."

Everyone laughed, including an exhausted Nadine.

"But I am sure the baby will be gorgeous," said Tatum.

Nadine waved her hands. "Enough about the baby! Why are you two hussies here? And on a weeknight?"

"We can't visit our best friend?" asked Alisa. "But really, it was Tatum's idea."

Nadine smirked in Tatum's direction. "I knew it. It must be serious, because you brought tequila knowing I can't have any. I appreciate the tacos."

"We can make you a virgin drink. We brought sparkling grape juice!" Tatum smiled, pulling out the bottle from the bag.

"I'd rather not even tease myself." Nadine eased

herself into the breakfast nook. "Never mind. I'll take the grape juice. Bring those tacos and stuff over here because I am not getting back up for a while."

Alisa mixed up some margaritas for her and Tatum and an enormous glass of sparkling grape juice for Nadine while Tatum piled their plates high with of beans, rice, guacamole, and fish tacos. They made their way to the breakfast nook. Nadine looked on and gave a satisfied nod as she picked up a taco and took a bite.

"Oh my god! So good," she said between bites. "Eddie won't let me have anything good and greasy! He's driving me nuts!"

Tatum laughed. "He's just looking out for you. Besides, word on the street is you two are driving each other nuts, including Alex."

"That freaking Alex! She exaggerates," Nadine laughed. "She is just trying to get used to the idea of not being a spoiled only child."

Alisa craned her neck looking around the kitchen. "Can you blame her? I mean look around? A mansion? Rich ex-basketball player step-daddy? I'd want this all to myself too."

"Hey! I made my own money too. Did you forget I was a CEO of one of the largest pharmaceutical companies in the country? All of this isn't Eddie!" whined Nadine.

Tatum and Alisa looked at each other with sly smiles. "My bad, superwoman," said Tatum. "Yeah, you were a boss babe."

"Shoot I still am!" Nadine rubbed her belly. "And when this baby comes, I am going back to work."

"Really? Why? Girl, if I had all this, I wouldn't touch another head of hair ever again!" Alisa said, pouring her second margarita.

"I enjoy being my own woman. I like having an identity outside of being Eddie Moody's wife, you know? I want to reclaim myself."

Tatum nodded. "I know what you mean. After Frankie died, going back to work actually helped me. Centered me."

"Is that the only thing centering you?" Alisa cut her eyes over her drink at Tatum.

Nadine looked back and forth between them, confused. "I feel like I am not in on the joke or something. What's up?"

Tatum put down her taco and pushed her plate away. "You're going to think this is the craziest shit in the world."

"No crazier than a forty-two-year-old woman having a baby... So, try me." Nadine took a bite of her taco, folded her arms, and put her feet up on the extra chair, awaiting an answer.

Tatum took a big gulp of her margarita.

"Remember how I told you I barely made it home in time for Frankie's transition? Well, I didn't tell you where I was…well…where *we* were…"

Alisa folded her arms and Nadine leaned in, as far as she could with her belly bump in the way.

"Well, Alisa and I went to Secrets…"

Nadine frowned. "The sex club? Why?"

"Because Frankie asked me to."

Nadine's eyes grew wide. "Say what now?"

"He wanted me to have some fun since he couldn't anymore," sighed Tatum. "And I was going to but…it didn't happen."

"Um, why not?'

"Cause Cassidy was a cockblocker," interrupted Alisa.

Nadine frowned. "Cassidy? What does he have to do with anything?"

Tatum cut her eyes to Alisa, who simply shrugged. "He was at the club. He told me to go home. Little did I know…"

"That he was a cockblocking hater," interrupted Alisa. Again.

Tatum frowned, annoyed. "Do you want to tell the story or let me do it?"

Alisa threw up her hands. "My bad. Go on."

"Anyway, I didn't go through with it. Cassidy pulled me in a room and threatened me and told me to go home. After the funeral, Cassidy and the guys said they wanted to talk to me."

"About what?" asked Nadine. "Was it about Frankie? The firm?"

Tatum's stomach roiled. She hadn't told Alisa any part of this crazy story, and she damn sure didn't need Nadine's judgmental and slightly prudish ass making faces at her. Tatum rolled her margarita glass around in her hand and stared at the ceiling as she spoke. "Months before his death, Franklin asked the guys to promise that they'd take care of me."

Alisa stared at Tatum with narrowed eyes. "Wait? This was Franklin's idea? Take care of you *how*?"

Tatum swallowed. "In every way...."

Nadine's mouth was now open as she held a taco in her hand "In every way meaning...sexually?"

Tatum nodded.

"Bitch! You didn't tell me that! Is that why Cassidy was quick to tell you to leave Secrets? Because he wanted to fuck you?" asked Alisa. "Explains why he turned me down."

"Wait? Are you supposed to fuck all three of them?" asked Nadine, baffled.

"No! Please stop saying 'fuck.' I don't think it's *just* about sex... You guys, I just don't think Franklin was thinking straight toward the end. That's all."

"Well, obviously!" said Nadine. "First off, what

dying man would tell his wife to get her kicks at a sex club and then ask his friends to fuck her when he's gone? Yeah. That was definitely the cancer getting to Franklin."

"Frankie and I used to go to Secrets all the time, before Morgan was born."

"Damn!" Nadine said as she shoveled some rice onto her fork. "And you think you know your friends."

Alisa shrugged. "Right! Man, I thought Frankie was a square. I guess I was wrong."

"So," Nadine said with a mouthful of rice and beans. "If it isn't about sex, then what's it about? Dating? Making sure you don't date?"

Tatum pinched the bridge of her nose. "I don't know. Maybe? But I think Franklin thought that his best friends were the best men he knew to look after me after his death. And... maybe he'd save me the pain of getting back out there."

"I see," said Alisa and Nadine in unison.

The trio sat in silence for several minutes, eating and drinking and munching on tortilla chips until Alisa pushed her plate away.

"Listen, I'd fuck them," declared Alisa. "All three of them. Especially that Cassidy."

Nadine nearly spit out her grape juice. "You

wouldn't! And Tate wouldn't either! Frankie hasn't even been dead three months!"

"There is no set time on mourning, Nadine! Tate has a whole lot of life in front of her. She's still fine and can get anyone. But obviously, Franklin also knew his wife. Maybe he knows something we don't. So, I say let them spoil you. Fuck you. Whatever. Life is short."

Nadine pursed her lips. "So, she's supposed to fuck all three at the same time?"

"Hell, if she wants to. Tatum has three holes."

"You're gross, Alisa," said Nadine with a laugh as she threw a wadded-up napkin across the table. Alisa playfully dodged.

Tatum knew Nadine would be freaked out. "Listen, Nadine, this is why I didn't want to tell you. I know this isn't your thing."

Nadine sighed. "It's not, but…I am trying to understand why you'd want to entertain such a foolish request. And who's to say they aren't making it up!"

"They aren't. I heard it from the horse's mouth. Franklin left a recording, asking them to take an oath to care for me after he was gone."

"That's a crazy ass oath," declared Nadine. "So, obviously you said no."

Tatum chewed her bottom lip. "I haven't decided."

"Oh, really?" Alisa gave Tatum a smirk. "And why are you in limbo?"

Tatum drained the last of her margarita, feeling tipsy, which gave her some courage. "I guess because maybe I am a little turned on at the idea that my husband thought so much of my needs, even in *his* time of need, that he'd go these lengths to keep me satisfied. "

"And I mean, it helps that Miles, Deacon, and Cassidy are fine as hell," interjected Alisa.

"Wait, I thought Miles was married?" asked Nadine. "And I thought Deacon was gay!"

"Um, Miles and Paula are divorced. Have been for a while now. And I don't think Deacon is gay." Tatum wasn't entirely sure about Deacon's sexuality, but she knew he was always entertaining good-looking men and women. "Maybe bisexual, but not gay."

"He's greedy then," huffed Nadine.

Alisa rolled her eyes hard. "Nadine, grow the fuck up! It is the twenty-first century. Some men are bisexual. Get with the program!"

"I say you do it, Auntie Tatum," declared Alex as she came around the kitchen. "You can be with as many men as you want."

"Stay out of grown folks' business!" Nadine yelled. "You aren't too old for me to snatch you up by the puff!"

"No, let the girl talk," said Alisa. "Gen Z has a different perspective these days."

Alex, seemingly feeling very adult and included, perched herself on the barstool at the island. "Auntie Tatum, life is short. And if you want to date women…men….a *bunch* of men at the same time… There is nothing stopping you. Uncle Frankie is gone. He's not coming back. And he would want you happy. Because he loved you so much. Don't feel bad because the idea of going out with other men sounds appealing."

"Well, isn't she wise!" said Alisa looking at Nadine. Nadine simply folded her arms atop her belly and huffed.

"Really, genius? And how is she supposed to date three men at once!" Nadine asked Alex.

Alex stuffed her mouth with a salsa-drench tortilla chip and shrugged. "I mean, they got these things called calendars. She can prioritize and schedule. Like she does her classes! She can rotate dates, heck, they can all go out on group dates. And if the vibes are there…"

Nadine held up her hand. "That is enough! I don't

want to hear my barely-young adult child talking about group sex."

"Who said anything about group sex?" cried Alex. "But, now that you mention it, Auntie Tate, make sure you get some clean STI reports and strap up. STIs are still on the rise in older Black women."

Tatum, Alisa, and Nadine all swiveled their necks in Alex's direction, slightly horrified that she mentioned STIs, strapping up, and "older" in the same sentence. The girl threw up her hands with a laugh, taking a container of guacamole and chips. "I see I've said too much. I'm going upstairs to watch the game with Eddie!"

"You better!" yelled Nadine in her direction as she shook her head at her child. When Alex was out of earshot, Nadine continued. "That crazy daughter of mine has a point, Tatum. You need to be careful out here."

Tatum laughed. "Well, one thing's for certain. I won't be getting pregnant. I had my tubes tied after Morgan."

"That's good, because one of them may have a breeding kink, and we don't need that!" said Alisa. Nadine, all out of napkins, threw a tortilla chip at Alisa.

"Why do you have to be so nasty?"

"Hey! Watch it! You coulda put my eye out!" Alisa

laughed as she dodged the chip. She looked her at Tatum, whose face was contorted. "What's wrong, Tatum?"

Tatum tugged at the bottom of her skirt. "What if I told y'all I had phone sex with Miles on FaceTime the other night?"

Both of their mouths flew open.

"When?" Nadine asked.

"And did it lead to some actual sex?" asked Alisa.

"The night of the big thunderstorm. And no. No actual sex," answered Tatum. "But it was really… nice. A little sexy. I was scared and alone. I missed Franklin. And Miles was there for me. He even sent flowers afterwards."

"Oh, a gentleman and a freak!" declared Alisa. "I like him."

"What about Cass and Deacon? Have you talked to them?" Nadine asked, pouring the last of her grape juice.

"I got a text from Deacon. Just being friendly. And Cassidy…" Tatum paused. The last time she saw Cassidy he was on his knees, apologizing. "Well, I haven't spoken to him since they met with me after the funeral."

Alisa poured the last of the margaritas. "So, he's the mysterious one? Interesting."

Tatum scratched her head, twirling a loose curl around her finger. "This is insane, right?"

"I don't think so," Alisa said. "Seems fun."

"Well, I do," said Nadine. "Seems dangerous. And what if Morgan finds out?"

To that question, Alisa gave a pointed finger of solidarity with Nadine. Tatum furrowed her brow. "Why would Morgan find out? What I do is my business! I'm not in his business."

"Um, you can't keep a secret from Mo! He's going to find out. And how the hell are you going to explain you fucking all three of his godfathers?" Nadine laughed as she polished off the last taco.

"Well, when you put it like that..." Tatum confessed. "It sounds pretty sleezy."

"I don't think it has to be," said Alisa. "I think you can make it however you want it to be."

Nadine reached across the table as far as she could and squeezed Tatum's hand. "Just be careful. Your heart is still fragile and vulnerable. I don't want you to get hurt three times as bad because of this."

After getting her fill of food and laughter at Nadine's, Tatum made her way home, taking the scenic route back to her house to give herself time to think. Between the flash of trees and lights, she thought about Franklin. The last time they danced in the park at the jazz fest. The last time they took a trip to Cabo. The last time they made vigorous love. The last time he looked at her and closed his eyes for his eternal rest.

The past two years had been dedicated to Franklin. She didn't, and couldn't, think of anything else.

Tatum thought about Nadine's words of being careful and Alisa wanting her to have some fun. She could do both. Right?

"Hey Siri, text Deacon, Miles, and Cassidy."

Tatum waited to be prompted to compose her text.

"Let's talk. Drinks at Paradiso. 8 p.m. Friday."

The assistant replied. "Would you like to send?"

As Tatum turned onto her street and into her driveway, she waited a beat before answering. "Yes. Send."

8

PARADISO

riday, Paradiso was packed as usual. Billows of cigar smoke and the smell of bourbon hung in the air. Tatum didn't mind the smell of either. She stood at the end of the long mahogany bar, scoping out where the fellas were sitting. She took a quick look at herself in the mirror behind the bar. She wore her hair up in a lazy bun with a few wispy hairs framing her face, black stilettos that Franklin bought on their anniversary in Paris, and a black bandage dress that she hadn't worn in years. Tatum was surprised that it still fit.

Tatum sauntered past a few tables until she came upon the corner table with Miles, Deacon, and Cassidy. Deacon looked up from his drink first, his lips curling into a smile.

"Damn, Tatum. You trying to give us a heart attack?"

Miles and Cassidy broke off their conversation and looked her way. Miles peered at her over his glasses, giving her body the once-over. Cassidy just stared at Tatum's face, his gaze piercing. Miles got up and pulled a chair out for Tatum.

"You did something different with your hair," Cassidy said.

Tatum put her hand to her hair. "Is it bad?"

"Not at all," Cassidy smiled. "I like it. It shows more of your beautiful face."

Tatum felt heat creep up her neck and to her cheeks. "I need a drink."

Deacon flagged down a waiter and ordered Tatum a glass of white wine. She could have used something stronger but thought twice about it. She needed to be as clear and levelheaded with them as she could.

Tatum fidgeted with the stem of her glass. "Thanks for meeting me. I wanted to talk about everything."

Miles leaned forward. "Sure. We're all ears." Deacon and Cassidy also gave her their full attention, sliding phones in pockets and finishing their respective drinks.

Tatum blew out a cleansing breath. "Frankie was

everything to me. My sun, and I was just rotating around him. I hadn't been with another man in twenty-three years, and now you're...well...*he's* asking me to give the three of you a shot. It seems outlandish and a hell of a way to get back out there."

Deacon laughed. "I feel you. But like we said, this is on you, Tatum. We respect your wishes above all else."

Cassidy reached out and gently touched the top of Tatum's hand. A shiver went down to her finger-tips. "Yeah, Tate, we are following your lead. Period."

"Okay." Tatum took another sip of wine. "First off, I want to be clear that I think this is a little crazy. So, we need to establish some rules."

"Go on," encouraged Miles. "What rules?"

"First, I know you all, but I don't *know* you. I have to get to know you."

Miles and Deacon both frowned. Cassidy took a sip of his beer, annoyed.

"I am not trying to offend you, but all the times we've interacted, it's been with Frankie present. We've never been alone. So, what I know about you all is through Frankie. I mean, Miles and Deacon, I've known you the longest, since you all had the firm together. Miles was married most of that time. But Cassidy, I don't know you that well.

You've been in the fellas' lives for what? Maybe six or seven years? What do you do for a living?"

To that, Miles and Deacon turned their attention to Cassidy, curious what his answer would be. Cassidy rolled his eyes. "I work for the government."

Tatum squinted. "That's it?"

Cassidy let out a raucous laugh. "I'll tell you on our date."

A date? That answer didn't bother anyone at the table but Tatum. She thought it best to move on. "Second, whatever this arrangement is, it can only last the summer. I don't need Morgan finding out about any of this."

"Why would Morgan know any of this?" asked Miles, scratching his bald head.

"He's my son! He's... I don't keep secrets from him. I never have."

"You never know, Morgan could be understanding." Miles continued as he flagged a waiter down to order another round of drinks, "He's a pretty open and liberal young man."

Tatum shook her head. "No. He sees you guys as his uncles. His godfathers. This would be a lot, even for liberal-minded Morgan."

"But," interrupted Deacon, "Wouldn't he want you happy? No matter how that looked?"

Tatum stared at Deacon. "Of course, but..."

"What if you want more than a summer?" asked Cassidy. "What if *we* want more than a summer? I know we could give you more." The way he asked made Tatum's skin heat and prickle.

"It can't. It won't." She declared. "A summer of this arrangement is all I can muster."

The three men looked at each other and nodded. "Anything else?" asked Miles.

"Yes," said Tatum as she sat straight up in her chair. "We'll schedule dates. Rotate a few weekends here and there. Maybe we all go out together sometimes."

What am I saying, Tatum thought. What would it look like being on a date with three men? She looked around the table. She presumed something a lot like this.

"So, do we need to sync our calendars or something?" asked Deacon with a laugh.

Tatum waved her hand. "It doesn't have to be that formal. We'll just keep an open line of communication."

"Communication is key. It's not just about going out or taking care of you," said Miles. "It is about having someone to lean on. You have us for that. No one else."

Tatum raised a brow. "No one?"

"Trust me, you won't need anyone else," said Cassidy, confidently.

Tatum's teeth sunk hard into her bottom lip. "Um. Okay."

The drinks arrived, and each one of them picked up their booze of choice.

Miles held up his glass. "To Franklin."

Tatum gave a tight smile, echoing, "To Franklin!" followed by a clanking of their glasses and beer bottles. She drank her wine, peering over the rim. She couldn't believe she was toasting her dead husband while entertaining the thought of dating his best friends.

"Well, we need something from you too, Tatum," said Deacon.

Tatum put down her drink slowly. "It depends. What is it?"

"For you to just relax. Be open. Have fun. Again, we got you." Deacon reached across the table for Tatum's hand. She freely gave it to him as he interlocked his fingers with hers. He had the softest hands and a perfect manicure, she observed. "Trust us, okay?"

Tatum nodded. "Okay."

"So, when do these dates start?" asked Miles.

Tatum smiled. "I guess this can count as the first date. A group date."

"Well, that's wack," laughed Deacon. "But I understand."

"And as for these dates," asked Cassidy, "Do we get to plan them or what?"

Tatum shrugged. "Sure. Honestly, I've never been much of a planner of dates. All I want is just some time alone to get to know you all as individuals, apart from what I knew of you via Frankie."

"And if it gets...*physical*?" asked Miles with some hesitation.

Tatum swallowed, thinking about her phone session just a week ago with Miles. But she also thought about young Alex's wise words. "When I am ready, we need STI tests. Clean bills of health. Medications you are on. No illicit drugs. If you're sleeping with other people, strap up. Hell, do that anyway."

All of their eyes landed on Deacon. He looked up from his phone. "What? Oh, was that for me? That's not cool. I use protection faithfully. Well, almost faithfully. But I am good. I'm also on PreP. People know the deal."

They all laughed. Tatum smiled. "Well, good to know. And I haven't been with anyone but Franklin. Unless..." Her eyes went sad.

Miles put a hand on her arm. "Hey. Frankie never stepped out on you. Real talk. Remember how you said he was your sun? I think you got it twisted. You were definitely his center. Holding him down. You were everything, baby girl."

A tear fell from Tatum's eyes. "Thanks. I just… You never know, y'know?"

"Never," reiterated Deacon. "And trust me, I tried to get him to be a little bad a time or two. He didn't, and he wouldn't. He loved you."

"No doubt," said Cassidy quietly. "So never think that he didn't."

Tatum nodded. "Okay." She dried her eyes with the end of her cocktail napkin, taking time to compose herself. The music in Paradiso picked up as the DJ spun some current tunes and a few people filed out on the lounge's dance floor. Tatum looked at her face in her compact and shook off her feelings.

"So," she started. "Since this is a date and all, who's going to take me for a spin on the dance floor?"

Miles threw up his hands with a laugh. "I am terrible at dancing."

Cassidy shook his head. "Nah, man, I am no dancer."

"Guess that'll be me," said Deacon. "These fools can't dance. C'mon, girl! Let me see you work it in this badass dress."

"Don't rub on my booty!" teased Tatum as she shimmied out of her chair, taking Deacon's hand.

"I'll make no promises," laughed Deacon. "Fellas, I'll bring her back in one piece."

Miles and Cassidy lifted their drinks as they watched Tatum and Deacon head to the dance floor, her laughter bouncing between the beats.

9

STARS DON'T COMPARE

When Tatum made it back home, her legs were sore as hell and her hair had been sweated out. She'd had a great time with the guys at Paradiso. After Deacon bumped and grinded on her around the floor to the faster songs, Miles stepped in for a few slow jams. His hands rested at her hips at a respectable angle until she felt comfortable. Once he felt a shift in her comfort, Miles pulled their bodies close, so close that Tatum could feel his heart beating through his vest. She wasn't sure if he was nervous, anxious, or excited. After a while, it was the only rhythm she could focus on.

Cassidy had opted to not dance with her. Instead, when she complained that her foot was sore, he gently lifted her foot out of her stiletto, into his lap, and rubbed the arch unabashedly at the table. He didn't care. His hands were firm, giving all the right pressure to all the right spots as if he knew reflexology. At one point, Tatum was sure that she moaned, which only made Cassidy more focused on the job of relieving her pressure, all with a satisfied smile.

She could have stayed there all night, laughing, talking, and drinking. But it was nearly four in the morning, and she thought it best she get home. She didn't need her lonely heart making any rash decisions.

Once safe inside, Tatum sent a group text and told them she'd had a lot of fun and that she'd be in touch. Barely able to wiggle out of her dress, Tatum was too exhausted to wash off her makeup or take a shower. She found pleasure in the feel of her sore and sweaty body. It was the most fun she'd had in months. Tatum crashed on the bed in her underwear, covering herself with her duvet.

The sun was barely up when her phone's text alerts woke Tatum. It was from Nadine and Alisa.

NADINE

Girl what happened?

ALISA

Did you sleep with them? One of them? All of them?

Tatum rolled her eyes and sat up in bed. Was that all they cared about? She didn't feel like texting them back. Instead, she showered and relaxed her sore muscles. Walking into her massive master bath made Tatum feel sad. She hadn't bothered to clean out Franklin's side of the bathroom. All of his razors, cologne, and aftershave were still there. She picked up a bottle of the aftershave and inhaled. God, he smells so good. Well, he used to smell so good.

Tatum turned on the shower as hot as she could stand it and let the water envelope her. She inhaled the steam and washed with her favorite body soap until she felt satisfied. After moisturizing herself and brushing her wet hair into a low bun to dry, Tatum wrapped herself in her robe and walked to her kitchen. An eerie feeling came over Tatum. The house was so quiet. No whirring of Franklin's machines, or the timbre of Morgan's booming but gentle voice. No after-funeral mourners.

It was just Tatum.

Alone.

After sleeping until midday, Tatum decided she'd try to figure out her new French press. As she was reaching for the coffee, her doorbell rang. Startled, she looked at the doorbell app on her phone. She wasn't expecting anyone on a Saturday morning, and anyone with sense would call. When she looked at the app, she could only see broad shoulders wearing a leather jacket. When the face glanced up in the camera, Tatum swallowed.

Cassidy.

Even in shades, with the beard and leather jacket, he looked every bit the part of a rebel. He was incredibly sexy.

Tatum didn't bother to communicate with him via the doorbell app; instead, she adjusted her robe and made her way to the front door. Slowly, Tatum opened it a crack.

"So, was calling out of the question?" Tatum asked as she leaned against her doorframe.

"Get dressed. I'm taking you to breakfast?" Cassidy commanded.

Tatum rolled her eyes, mildly irritated. "Excuse me?"

"Breakfast, Tate. I'm sure you haven't eaten in a while. It'll sober you up."

Tatum scratched her head. "I am sober. I think…"

It wasn't until Cassidy sighed that Tatum noticed that he was holding a motorcycle helmet.

"Oh, hell no! I am not getting on a death contraption with you, Cass!" Tatum had only been on a motorcycle once in her lifetime, and she'd been terrified because the guy wanted to race with her on the back. She'd vowed never again to ride a motorcycle, no matter how fine the man attached to it was.

Cassidy looked down at his helmet, a glimmer of a smile forming. "I'm an expert Tatum. Been riding for decades. Trust me, okay? I'd never hurt you. So, let's get some breakfast and do a little riding while the weather is good."

Tatum's lips formed a tight scowl, to which Cassidy gently pulled her chin between his thumb and index finger. His eyes focused squarely on the place where her bottom lip gently grazed his thumb.

"Don't do that, mama. I'm a little sick and tired of you frowning at me."

Was he always so goddamn demanding? Tatum let out a slow release of air and backed away. "I'll be a few minutes. Let me get dressed."

It took Tatum about ten minutes to throw on some jeans, ankle boots, and a long-sleeved V-neck shirt. She threw her stuff in a small crossbody bag, and for the sake of time, only had on gloss, mascara, and groomed brows. Cassidy looked her up and down. Tatum wasn't sure if he approved of her look or not, but she didn't bother asking.

After a quick lesson on getting on and off his motorcycle, Cassidy put a helmet over Tatum's head, adjusting the straps under her chin. It was way heavier than she expected, and Tatum wasn't sure how she'd balance herself.

"Just hold tight around my waist and follow me as I move. I'll do the rest," Cassidy assured her.

Tatum positioned her hands around Cassidy. He was thick and firm, and even under the leather jacket, she could feel every cut of his abs and obliques. Cassidy took a gloved hand and moved Tatum's hand closer to his body.

"Tighter," he instructed.

Tatum said nothing and did was she was told. Seemed like she was always in the habit of obeying him.

Cassidy was a superb driver. He didn't go too fast, but he certainly knew how to handle curves and tricky inclines. Tatum was worried their combined weight was going to be too much, but if it was, Cassidy didn't make it seem as if he was straining one bit. It was if she were as light as a bag of sugar on the back of his bike.

Once Tatum got over the initial nerves, the ride itself was exhilarating. Feeling the wind under her shirt and nip at her collar was amazing. Speeding past cars and in and out of traffic was also pretty dope. At the stoplight, Tatum leaned down, her face dangerously close to Cassidy's neck. He smelled like sweat, leather, and something like myrrh. It was earthy and warm. Under the early morning skies, Cassidy smelled like summer.

When they finally came to a complete stop and Tatum got off the motorcycle, she took off her helmet and looked around. She realized she was at Marion's on the River, a pretty posh brunch spot in the city. She looked down at her jeans and boots, unsure if she was dressed for caviar and champagne brunches. As if he could read her mind, Cassidy took the helmet from her, fixing a flyaway strand of hair that was in her face.

Cassidy trailed his finger along her temple. "You're fine."

Tatum bit her lip. "Cass, I am in jeans."

"I said you're fine. Trust me." They walked up to the hostess stand where the gorgeous, modelesque hostess greeted Cassidy with a huge smile.

"Mr. Valentine. Wonderful to see you again. Your usual table?" she asked as she gathered the menus.

"Yes, Tessa. The usual table."

Puzzled, Tatum turned to look at Cassidy. "Mr. Valentine?"

Cassidy gave Tatum an equally puzzling look. "What? Don't you remember my last name?"

"That's not it and you know it! You must be pretty important to have a regular table here."

Cassidy let out a low laugh. "You're hilarious."

Tatum and Cassidy squeezed past the waiting crowd, following the hostess toward their table. Tatum noticed the eyes of the women following Cassidy, clad in leather and jeans and a basic white t-shirt. They were salivating over a man who didn't even bother to look their way. His hand rested on her lower back the entire time.

Their table was on the patio overlooking the river, with a bucket of champagne and a carafe of orange juice already there. Cassidy pulled out Tatum's chair before sitting down. The waitress left the menus, running down the specials before pouring them sparkling water.

"Do you kidnap women all the time and take them to breakfast?" asked Tatum as she folded her napkin in her lap.

"Kidnap? I recall you leaving willingly."

"You sure about that? I mean, you had so much bass in your voice it sounded more like a command."

Cassidy looked over the menu at Tatum. "Sometimes I can't help it."

Tatum laughed. "Oh, I believe you. You had me shook at Secrets."

Cassidy leaned closer, his hand touching the top of Tatum's. "I'm still sorry about that. Trust me. I get a little protective sometimes."

Tatum looked down at Cassidy's hand, his fingers stroking the tops of her knuckles. His fingers were surprisingly soft, and Tatum could feel her own fingers tremble. "So, a standing reservation at Marion's, Mr. Valentine?" Tatum slowly removed her hand, trying to change the subject. "Fancy!"

Cassidy smiled. "I come here just about every Saturday. Especially if I've been working late."

"Alone?" asked Tatum before she could stop herself.

Cassidy leaned back in his chair. "That's not the question you want to ask."

Tatum felt caught in a lie. "What are you talking about?"

"You want to know how many women I bring to my standing reservation at Marion's. The answer is none that matter. Until now."

Tatum stammered. "I...I wasn't concerned about that."

Cassidy winked. "Right."

At that moment, the waitress appeared to take their order. Tatum ordered the eggs Benedict with crab cakes and potatoes, and Cassidy ordered lobster and caviar omelet. Everything looked divine. They settled into casual conversation, with Tatum mostly talking about Morgan and how proud she was of him. Cassidy politely nodded between bites, but

Tatum could tell that he didn't want to spend the entire brunch talking about his godson.

Tatum moved her potatoes around her plate. "I feel like even though you've been in my life for a while, I don't know you."

Cassidy wiped the corners of his mouth. "That's perfect. Because this brunch is for you to get to know me. Ask me anything."

"Okay, so what do you do for a living? Are you a spy? An assassin?" She dropped her voice to a whisper. "A drug cartel boss?"

"What?" Cassidy let out a deep, rumbling laugh. "First, I hate the sight of blood, and as big as I am, I'd be terrible at sneaking around. Second, I don't do drugs. Not even weed."

Tatum gestured her hands toward Cassidy. "I mean with the tattoos, beard, and the grill. I just assumed it wasn't something legal."

Cassidy took a sip of his mimosa with a smirk. "Plenty of people do. But my actual job is probably a lot more surprising."

"Which is?"

Cassidy leaned in close, to which Tatum followed suit. "I look for aliens."

Tatum's eyes grew wide. "Say what now?"

Cassidy laughed, a hint of playful mischief coloring his soft, round face. "I am kidding. I'm an astrophysicist. BS from A&T, PhD from Stanford. But I do work for the government. It's called NASA."

Tatum nearly choked. "Are you serious?" Tatum's eyes roamed over Cassidy. Nothing about the man said scientist, let alone astrophysicist. "Why is it that the fellas acted as if they knew nothing about your career? They always joked that you have a mysterious job. Or no job at all."

Cassidy rolled his eyes. "They know. They just zoned out when I talk about black holes or collapsing stars. They probably think I'm talking about an episode of *Star Wars*."

"Wow," Tatum said. "I'm intrigued. I would have never thought." Intrigued was putting it mild. It turned Tatum on because Cassidy looked like a gangster but was an academic. She'd met no one like him. She could see how he and Franklin became friends.

Cassidy shrugged. "I know. But I do have a brain. After I got injured playing basketball, I figured I was good at math and I loved science. No more athletic scholarship, so let me parlay an academic one."

"That was really smart."

"I am not changing who I am just because I'm an academic. So, I'mma wear the grills, dunks, and ride my bike. I still like hood shit. And I will fuck someone up. But I love my job. Actually, if you let me, I want to take you somewhere after brunch."

Tatum smiled. "I'd love that."

Tatum and Cassidy talked for hours. She learned he was an only child, still close to his elderly parents that he took care of. He was allergic to strawberries. And when Tatum asked if he read science fiction, Cassidy's eyes lit up as he talked about his favorite works by N.K. Jemisin, Nisi Shawl, and Octavia Butler, even talking about how it informed his own work. Tatum's geeky heart nearly exploded.

Once they were done with brunch, Tatum hopped on the back of Cassidy's bike as they zoomed through the city. She was much more relaxed as she held on to Cassidy, letting the wind hit her face and the sunlight bathe her exposed bits of skin. She was so relaxed, feeling a sense of peace she hadn't felt in a while, that she nearly closed her eyes as they rode. It wasn't until the bike made an abrupt stop that she knew they had reached their destination.

Tatum removed her helmet and slowly dismounted from the motorcycle. They were at the observatory and planetarium in Druid Hills. "What are we doing here?"

Cassidy removed his helmet, still on the bike. Tatum's eyes went straight to his thick, jean-clad thighs. She swallowed, pressing her own thighs together. Alisa was right.

This man was sho'nuff fine as hell.

"I figured I'd take you to see the second most beautiful thing in the world that consumes my thoughts."

Tatum frowned. "Second?"

Cassidy got off the bike, closing the space between them with quick strides. He took Tatum by the hand, staring at her with whiskey-colored eyes. "Yes, second. Come on."

The planetarium was nearly empty. Cassidy led Tatum toward the back-middle row of seats. Tatum looked around, feeling self-conscious; she couldn't remember the last time she'd been in the dark with a man. Cassidy must have sensed her nerves. He reached for her hand, stroking it.

Tatum nervously giggled. "Damn, last time I was here was on a field trip with Morgan's fifth grade class. Not sure what we watched. Stars, duh. Or maybe it was about dinosaurs. He loved dinos back then. And…"

"Relax, Tate. You're babbling. It's just me." Cassidy laughed, kissing the top of her knuckles and sending a sizzle down her wrist.

Tatum swallowed. She felt her neck heating from embarrassment. "Right. Sorry."

They continued to watch the show as Cassidy pointed out several things. Tatum was intrigued and tried to listen intently, but found it hard to concentrate because he smelled so incredible. Like the leather of his jacket, sweat, and woods.

"If it were dark out," began Cassidy, "I'd take you over to the observatory so you could see the constellations in action. But this will have to do."

Tatum smiled. "No, it's perfect."

The lights dimmed, and a voice boomed. Above their heads, the stars twinkled as the voice explained the constellations and planets. Tatum felt as if she was floating in the galaxy, untethered as they zoomed between the Milky Way.

"Do you think we are alone out here?" asked Tatum.

Cassidy shrugged. "I don't know. Probably not."

Tatum stared at the rings of Saturn, her eyes focused on the colors. "Sometimes I wish I was up there. Maybe I wouldn't be alone." The unspoken, "with Franklin," part was certainly implied.

"You're not alone. You've got me…and the rest of the fellas…" said Cassidy.

"But, Cass…I…"

"Shh," he admonished. "You can't be sad while looking at the beauty of the universe. Otherwise, I'm going to have to take your mind off things."

Tatum snorted. "Oh yeah, like what? Tell me about black holes."

"Now that you mentioned it," Cassidy leaned over closer, his lips and beard grazing the lobe of her ear. Suddenly, her panties were flooded with warmth and wetness. His large hand slid over her belly, to the top of her jeans, unbuttoning them. "I love black holes."

Tatum squirmed in her seat. "What are you doing?" She looked around. They were near the back of the planetarium with no one around them, but they were still in public. When she felt Cassidy's hand slide inside her pants, his fingers finding her wet folds, Tatum let out a hiss. She gripped the armrests as he slipped up and down her slit. "Cass, we shouldn't do this. Not here."

Cassidy shook his head, his lips still against the curve of her neck. "Quiet, Tatum," he whispered. "Be a good girl, mama, and let me take care of you." Tatum felt her pussy contract at his words, grasping at something that wasn't there yet she desperately craved.

"Just focus on the stars, baby." Cassidy licked up and down Tatum's neck while his fingers finally parted her folds, finding her clit. Cassidy rubbed the bundle of nerves until Tatum shook. She stared up at the ceiling as shooting stars and comets zipped by.

She felt herself getting close, as if she could join those heavenly bodies up in the sky.

"I saw the way you looked at my dick at Secrets," Cassidy whispered, not letting up on his assault on her clit, his lips tracing along her jawline. "I was so hard. You had on that yellow lingerie set that glowed against your skin. I wanted to bend you over and fuck you so badly. That young dude wasn't going to get this pussy." With that, Cassidy moved his attention from Tatum's clit, sliding two fingers inside her hot, already-drenched pussy. He worked his fingers until they were fully coated and soaked. "But I knew it wasn't time. I'm patient. I can wait."

Tatum bit her lip, trying to stifle her moans. "Cass, I am going to come," she panted, feeling tears form in the corners of her eyes. "Please." The last part came out in a hoarse whisper that she hoped no one in the planetarium heard.

Cass stopped moving his fingers but didn't remove them right away, relishing in the pulsing sensation her pussy did around them. Immediately, Tatum felt betrayed. "Not yet, Tate." He kissed her temple and removed his fingers from her panties, which were now soaked and sticking to the mound of her pussy like cling wrap. Out of the corner of her eye, she saw Cassidy lick his fingers, making her whimper.

Without warning, the lights came up and Tatum scrambled to button her jeans. Cassidy's jacket was over his lap, no doubt hiding an erection that she knew was present. He looked at her, the gleam of his bottom grill showing. "Did you enjoy the show?"

"You could have let me…" Tatum rolled her eyes, then grabbed her crossbody. "Never mind."

"What? Come?" Cassidy smirked, then rose, taking Tatum's hand. "I could have. But I'm a man of science. I already know it's going to take more than my fingers to get you off properly."

It was early evening when Cassidy dropped Tatum off at her doorstep. After the planetarium and riding around the city, they picked up a couple of Cuban sandwiches and sodas and sat in the park. Cassidy was a perfect gentleman. It was as if he hadn't had his fingers in Tatum's panties and jeans hours before. His bike rumbled, making a noise in the posh neighborhood where she lived. She looked around and saw neighbors peeking out their windows, trying to see what was making all the noise.

"They are watching," Tatum whispered, as she handed Cassidy her helmet.

"Then let's give them something to talk about." Cassidy gripped the bottom of Tatum's shirt, pulling her toward him. With the other hand, he tilted her chin upward, staring down at her lips. Tatum could feel her breathing quicken. And when Cassidy's lips touched hers, it only made Tatum breathe deeper to inhale him. His tongue parted her lips, his hands palmed her ass, and he kissed her until she was weak and breathless. His beard tickled the underside of her jawline and made her feel fluttery.

Finally, Cassidy broke the kiss, his teeth grazing her bottom lip for good measure, sending an electric current straight to Tatum's clit.

"Next time, I'll have to show you the stars at night. But they still won't compare to you."

Tatum nodded, unable to say anything else. She watched as Cassidy got on his bike and exited out of her driveway.

10

INTRUSIONS

atum stared out of the window, unable to grade the pile of essays that were on her desk. She thought about the past few weeks. Phone sex with Miles. Dancing with guys. The wind on Cassidy's bike. His fingers inside her. The thought made her pussy clinch and her nipples hard. Sadness replaced horniness. Not because she missed Franklin. That much was obvious. But because she hadn't realized how touch and attention-starved she had been during his illness. Now she was craving it. Demanding it.

And that was terrifying.

"Get it together, T," Tatum mumbled to herself, shaking the thoughts away as she ran her hands through her hair.

It had been years since she'd been touched and, in

124

a few weeks, these men had awakened something that she thought would remain dormant for the rest of her life. She thought that she'd be relegated to being a caregiver, either to Franklin or Morgan, and she was ok with that. Now, the spark of sexual desire was back. She wasn't sure she could handle it.

A knock at her door broke her out of her daydreams. She beckoned the person in, not bothering to turn around from her position.

"Dr. Simmons?"

Tatum turned to face her student, Jason. She smiled. In the past weeks, he'd been a hard-working student, albeit a touch scatterbrained. He was engaging in class, even if he didn't always understand the material. Tatum appreciated his efforts.

"Yes, Mr. Duggar. How can I help?"

Jason took a seat in front of her desk. "I got a B minus on this paper on Butler and I just wanted to know why. I mean, I thought it was solid."

Tatum motioned for Jason to hand her the paper. She browsed through her notes, careful to read several lines. Finally, she handed the paper back. "Jason, I do not think you expound enough on your argument that Octavia Butler was critical of motherhood in her works. I didn't see any sources cited that supported your argument. I thought it was strong, but I needed more."

Jason nodded. "It's just that I've never gotten less than an A on a paper. I was surprised. I thought maybe it was because…." He diverted his eyes from Tatum's, biting the inside of his lips.

Tatum frowned. "You thought what, Jason?"

He waved his hands. "Nothing. It's nothing."

"No, please say it." Although she asked, Tatum knew she'd regret it. The sinking feeling in her gut told her so.

"Because of the last time we saw each other. Well, the first time." Jason leaned back in his seat. Tatum watched the t-shirt on his body stretch across his chest, the faint outline of his nipple piercings visible through the thin fabric. Tatum quickly reminded herself to look at his face, anything to center herself.

Tatum decided it was safer to play dumb. "Not sure what you mean, Jason. You simply introduced yourself and apologized for missing class. No harm done."

Jason leaned closer, his voice lowered to a husky whisper. "No. At Secrets."

Tatum felt as if she was swallowing rocks. She blinked rapidly. "Not sure I follow."

"Aight, so you playing it like that?" Jason rolled his eyes, a smirk appearing on his face. "Listen, I get it. You're a professor, I'm a student, and that probably violates some kind of HR thing. I wouldn't dare tell anyone I saw you there. I wasn't expecting favoritism or anything. I just thought maybe you gave me this grade because you and I—"

Tatum held up her hand, cutting him off. "That's enough. Let me assure you I'd never grade based on anything going on in my personal life. This paper just wasn't good enough. Next time, cover all of your bases and arguments that you posit." Tatum switched her focus back to the papers on her desk, expecting him to leave. But Jason didn't move an inch.

"I supposed that's fair." Jason nodded, then looked up at her with eyes that were beyond heated. He chuckled to himself, which slightly unnerved Tatum. "I don't know why you thought I wouldn't remember your body. Or your smell. It's unforgettable." She watched as he palmed what appeared to be a growing hard-on in his pants.

Dear God, what was happening?

Tatum literally clutched the string of pearls on her neck. "Mr. Duggar, this conversation is making me uncomfortable. I'm going to ask you to leave."

Instead, Jason stood and approached Tatum. He pulled her chair underneath him, hovering over her. His erection directly in her face. Tatum's heart raced and her pussy betrayed her fear by contracting. He leaned down close to her face. "You stand in front of the class teasing me with what I could have had."

Tatum could smell his aftershave or cologne. It began to make her sick. She wanted to scream but her voice was trapped in a web of arousal and abhorrence.

"That guy pulled you away before I could do all the things I wanted to do to you." Jason continued, delicately pulling at the same string of pearls, examining them as if they were strange and foreign. He let his finger dip inside Tatum's damp cleavage and she gasped, shivering under his touch. "Look at you, nipples already hard. I wanted to lick your full tits, suck those hard brown diamonds in my mouth. I wanted to put my mouth on your clit and suck your fucking soul out and claim it." He moved her hand to his hardness, making her stroke its veiny length. "I wanted to fuck you with this hard dick and have you cream all over it. I wanted to watch it drip out of your tight little pussy."

Tatum swallowed and snatched her hand out of Jason's grasp. "Get out. Now," she said through gritted teeth. "Don't come back in my class for the rest of the summer." There was only a week left in the shortened summer semester. She could pass him along with the grade he had without ever seeing him again.

Jason moved back, a near-sinister grin on his lips. "It's fine, Dr. Simmons. I got what I wanted out of the class anyway." He looked down at Tatum's thighs as she pressed them together. "Well, almost everything. You're an excellent teacher."

With that, Jason left Tatum's office, leaving her there with a racing pulse and wet panties. She grabbed a bottle of water from her bag and downed it in seconds, wishing it was something stronger. She took several deep breaths, trying to compose herself. Her moment of attempted calm was disrupted when her phone began to vibrate.

"So, I heard everyone has had a solo date with you except me," said Deacon with a slight laugh in his voice.

Before she could say a word, Tatum burst out in tears. The call ended and Deacon called back via video. Tatum wiped her tears on her sleeve and answered.

"Tate, darling. What's going on?" Deacon was in his office at the firm. He got up and closed his door. "Do I need to call Miles? I think he's in a meeting but I can get him."

"No," assured Tatum, shaking her head. "It's nothing."

"It sure as hell doesn't sound like nothing. What's going on?"

Tatum took a shaky breath, recalling the strange

events of her afternoon to Deacon who, by the end of the call, was seething with anger.

"What's the little fucker's name, again?" Tatum could see the top of Deacon's curls as he reached for a pen to write it down.

Tatum wiped the sweat beading at her nape. "Jason Duggar."

"We'll handle it."

Tatum's eyes grew big. "Who is 'we?' Listen, he's harmless. I think. But I'm fine. I handled it."

"Exactly, you *think* he's harmless. You have no idea how a creep like that operates. Let us worry about it. In the meantime, you need to leave for the day."

Tatum stared at all the papers on her desk. "I can't. I have a ton of papers to grade."

"Those papers will be there tomorrow. I am calling my masseuse at Spa Denali. I'll tell her to squeeze you in."

Tatum frowned. "Deek, I can't just drop everything."

Deacon smiled and simply replied, "Be there at 3 p.m."

Then ended the call.

Deacon had been right. Greta, his masseuse, was just the thing that Tatum needed. She was so tense and hadn't done any self-care in months. Greta rubbed every single worry and care away, including her confrontation with Jason. When she was done, Tatum smelled like the finest of oils and was relaxed beyond measure.

When Tatum pulled into her driveway, she was surprised to see Deacon's car. She knew it was his because he was the only one of the fellas with vanity plates that read, "DeeksAudi." Deacon loved his cars as much as he loved sex. At least, that's what Frankie told Tatum when Deacon purchased a new ride every year. Franklin convinced her to give keys to his friends in the event that something happened. At first, she was leery at the idea of three dudes with keys to her sanctuary. True to their word, they never violated her space or did anything out of bounds. They were always respectful with the use of the key for emergencies, especially as Frankie's condition worsened.

Guess today constitutes an emergency, thought Tatum.

Tatum parked in the garage and came through the mudroom to the kitchen. The smell of garlic and peppers wafted through the air. She saw Deacon at her stove, dress sleeves rolled up, sautéing veggies in a pan. She smiled, a little more than grateful for a home-cooked meal. Other than leftovers or takeout, Tatum hadn't been in the mood to eat let alone cook. She sat at the island and folded her arms, enjoying the view.

Hearing her come in, Deacon looked over his shoulder and smiled. "You're home. Good." He came over and kissed Tatum on the cheek, as if he'd done it a million times. Tatum blushed at the thought of getting used to him in her space.

Deacon leaned against the island. "I take it Greta did her thing. You looked relaxed."

Tatum smiled. "She did. But I didn't know I was getting treated to dinner. The massage was more than enough, Deek. You didn't have to do all this."

"I wanted to. So, let me. Would you like a glass of wine?"

"I'd love that."

Tatum watched as Deacon moved about the kitchen. His slacks were fitted and tailored within an inch of their life. Deacon was the epitome of tall, dark, and handsome. He was well over six feet, with curly black hair that he managed to barely tame. His goatee was always perfectly manicured, and Tatum was more than jealous of the smoothness of his skin. He always smelled good and his hands were always soft. He was, in a single word, perfect. She could see how Deacon had women, and men, fawning all over him. Shit, she was salivating right now.

Deacon poured glasses of Pinot Grigio for both of them. He motioned for her to raise her glass for a toast.

Tatum squinted. "What are we toasting?"

Deacon shrugged. "Hell, I don't know. I just know I shouldn't pour a fine glass of wine without a toast."

"Touché," Tatum giggled, and she clinked her glass then took a sip. She tried to peer over Deacon's shoulder to see what he was cooking but couldn't tell. It looked like he was cooking for an army, not just the two of them.

"Can I do anything to help?" asked Tatum, coming around to see the ingredients.

"Hey now!" Deacon moved Tatum away, playfully obstructing her view. "I'm cooking. No need for you to get in my way. Listen, why don't you take that wine upstairs. Run a nice hot bath and continue relaxing. I may have a little surprise for you on your bed."

Tatum raised a brow. "First, you're in my kitchen and now you go to my bedroom. Oh, so you've just been all over my house making yourself at home, huh?"

Deacon laughed, swatting Tatum playfully with a dish towel. "Go. Now, T. I'm serious!"

"Are you?" Tatum pushed herself up on tip toes, trying to sneak around Deacon's large frame to pick up a spoon. Deacon body blocked her, gently pushing her into the pantry door with the weight of his frame.

Tatum laughed, then looked up into his eyes. They were cola brown and gorgeous, with flecks of gold around the irises. She tried not to stare, but it was impossible. Deacon dipped his head down, his chest pressing against her upturned chin. Tatum felt his large hand press against her hip to steady her. She swallowed, trying to regain her balance.

"Maybe I should take that bath," Tatum confessed in a whisper. If she stayed a moment longer, she had a feeling she and Deacon would be burning down the house. Literally and figuratively.

"Like I said," said Deacon in a low, gravelly voice. "Go relax. I'll finish dinner." He removed his hand from her hip as she slipped past him and headed upstairs.

When Tatum entered her bedroom, she found a gold and white-wrapped box on the bench in front of her bed. She was tempted to open it immediately, but decided to wait until after her Deacon-ordered bath.

Tatum quickly undressed, turned on some music, and poured luxury bath salts and oils into her tub. She pinned her hair up and slipped into the warm bubbles that engulfed her. She leaned against the bath pillow, humming along with the jazzy tunes until she felt herself fully loose and cotton-candy soft.

After twenty minutes of relaxing, Tatum found her favorite vanilla body oil and slathered herself until she shone. She brushed her silver-streaked hair into a low bun and did her skincare routine. Her face, over the past few years, gained a few more wrinkles. She stared at her naked body in the mirror, taking inventory of her stretch marks, cellulite, and hip dips. Her breasts were still large and heavy but sagged a bit. Despite the changes, men still found her to be desirable. The past weeks had proven that.

Tatum walked into her bedroom and sat on the bench, placing the box in her lap. She stared at it for a while until she opened it. On the delicate tissue paper inside was a card. She opened it and read it.

"Seasons change, darling.
— Deacon"

Tatum didn't exactly know what that meant, but she assumed it had to do with her and Frankie. She pulled back the tissue paper to find a sexy black satin nightgown with mesh paneling down the sides and middle. Tatum slipped into it and looked at herself in the full-length mirror. It hugged her every curve, the expansive swell of her breasts and her hips.

"I knew you'd look amazing in that."

Tatum turned to see Deacon standing in the doorway, hands resting on the top of the frame. He'd slipped out of his dress shirt altogether and was now wearing a white tank, slacks and bare feet. He moved to stand behind Tatum to also look at her in the mirror. He bent to kiss her exposed shoulder, making Tatum's flesh pebble.

Deacon's lips trailed over the curve of her neck to her jawline.

"Why are you doing all this?" asked Tatum as her head instinctively bent to allow Deacon room to explore.

Deacon lifted Tatum's bun and placed a chaste kiss at the nape of her neck. "You've had a terrible day. I'm taking care of you. It's what I'm supposed to do."

Tatum's giggle quickly morphed into a groan when Deacon's tongue traced the top of her spine. "Isn't this a bit over the top?"

"I asked myself what Frankie would want. Trust

me, this is nothing. Shit, he'd do more than this and you know it."

"I know," Tatum smiled. "Well, I appreciate that."

"Is there anything else you need to relax?" asked Deacon in a husky voice that was as sweet and thick cane syrup.

Tatum could feel his growing erection at her backside. The ache in her pussy signaled her need, and she had to do something, anything, to quench its thirst. She turned and pulled Deacon down for a kiss, her hands flying to catch on to his curls. Deacon's mouth danced with hers, painting his taste against her tongue and nipping at her bottom lip with his teeth. When Deacon sucked her tongue into his mouth, Tatum moaned, signaling Deacon to pick her up and take her to the bed.

"Let me make you feel good, Tate."

He sat her down at the edge, bending down on his knees. Slowly, he lifted the hem of her chemise up until it was bunched around her waist, exposing her pussy to the air. Tatum wasn't completely clean shaven because Frankie didn't care for that. Suddenly, she was hit with a touch of self-conscious-ness, but the look in Deacon's eyes told her to quiet those thoughts. He was ready to feast, no matter the presentation.

Deacon swiped a thumb through her slit and

sucked. "Fuck, you taste so good." He then took his finger, stretching her open wider as if to get a better look. Tatum was so turned on by his examination, her pussy involuntarily contracted over and over. Deacon wickedly smiled. "So pretty and pink. And she's winking at me. I think I need to properly introduce myself."

Deacon took the flat of his tongue and licked up Tatum's pussy, making her back arch off the bed. Deacon held her hips down, widening her thighs as his tongue continued its assault on her pussy. He licked inside her and out, the tip of his tongue teasing her clit.

"Fuck, Deek!" Tatum cried out, her hands clawing at his back. She could feel his lips curl into a smile against her thigh as he licked his way back up to her pussy. Deacon lifted the hood of her clit with his tongue and latched on, sucking her as if he had a point to prove. As if he was marking his place. The more Tatum moved, trying to catch her breath and gain leverage, the more Deacon sucked, pressing her into orgasms that seemed to roll into each other, one after another. Tatum was sure that she'd black out, die, and join Frankie in the afterlife.

Tatum lifted a bit on her elbows, angling herself to see Deacon go to work. When he looked up, eyes locking on hers, he finally lifted his head. His face was covered with an obscene amount of her arousal, and Tatum wanted to lick it off his beard, lips, and chin.

Deacon's hands were in his pants, stroking his dick. "You taste so fucking good, Tate. I can't get enough of you." With that, he dove back down to taste Tatum some more. Deacon had a playbook to her pussy. This was solidified when Deacon added fingers to the pussy eating equation, pushing at her G-spot with a fury. He knew exactly how to get her off. He'd been learning her body well.

Tatum tried to focus but couldn't "I…ohh, fuck… What…about…dinner?" asked Tatum as she felt another orgasm coming on.

"I'm having dinner now," Deacon laughed, giving Tatum a wicked lick to her clit that made her scream. "But I'm going to feed you, darling." Deacon gave Tatum one last lick to her inner thigh before pulling down her chemise.

Tatum watched as Deacon stood. "But you're still…" She nodded toward the bulge in his pants.

Deacon looked down, smoothing over his slacks. "Today has been about you. Not me." He leaned down and kissed Tatum's forehead. "We have plenty of time to get to that. But you're right. Man can't live off pussy alone. I hope you like chicken and sausage jambalaya and cornbread."

Tatum's stomach rumbled at the mention of food. Post-orgasm hunger had her at her most ravenous. "I do." Tatum stood, smoothing down her chemise. "Should I change for dinner?"

"Hell no," Deacon's eyes roamed over her body before leaving her bedroom. "I think our guests would appreciate how you look tonight."

Tatum brow furrowed. "Guests?"

11

DINNER GUESTS

Tatum made her way down the steps to find Miles and Cassidy in her kitchen. They both stopped mid conversation to look at her. Tatum's nipples tightened at their perusal of her body. She never got turned on this way in their presence, and now, one look made her hot. Miles came over first, kissing her cheek.

"She does look good in this, Deacon," he said, still staring at Tatum. "Doesn't she, Cass?"

Tatum's eyes met Cassidy's, and he looked like he wanted to rip the damn chemise off of her. "It's very nice," he said. "Deacon has good taste."

Tatum blushed as she sat at the kitchen island. "Well, I appreciate Deacon taking care of me today." Her thighs pressed together at the thought of how well he'd done.

141

Miles poured glasses of chardonnay for everyone except Cass, who had a glass of bourbon. "Well, it appears you look well taken care of." He slid the glass toward her with a wink, then handed the glass to Deacon, who kissed Miles on the cheek in appreciation.

Tatum's eyes widened at the softness and familiarity of the kiss. "I...uh...hold on." She motioned between Deacon and Miles. "Is there something I should know?"

"I swear I didn't say anything," said Deacon, holding his hands up.

Deacon and Miles looked at each other until Deacon nodded, giving Miles to the go-ahead to explain. "Deacon and I used to have a thing back at Central. Off and on. But we realized we were better off as friends."

Tatum smiled, realizing that explained their dynamics so much. They often acted like an old married couple versus best friends. "Did Frankie know this?"

Deacon laughed. "Who do you think caught us making out in the law library? Thankfully, he didn't trip. We were his best friends."

Frankie never told Tatum any of this, and she wondered why. It certainly wouldn't have changed her love for either of them. She assumed it had to do with Paula. The woman was unhinged. At first, she and Paula were cool. Then, suddenly, they weren't anymore. Tatum nodded. "Is this why you and Paula broke up?"

Miles waved his hands. "Absolutely not. Paula knew I was bi when we got married. No, we ended because she couldn't stop drinking and doing cocaine. She damn near snorted up our life's savings. She had her own demons to deal with. She liked Deacon, relatively speaking."

"Relatively speaking is the key word here," said Deacon, pointing his glass toward Miles. "I think part of her thought I was the reason for the divorce, but trust me, I wanted them to work it out. Besides, I don't mess with married folks, either. Too much baggage."

Tatum looked over at Cassidy, and before she could ask, he replied, "Nah, baby, I am into pussy only." His eyes looked at her over his rocks glass. "Right now, a specific pussy is looking really good."

Tatum nearly choked. "Jesus, Cass."

Cassidy shrugged with a wicked smile. "It's the truth."

Tatum watched as Deacon moved about the kitchen, plating jambalaya and cornbread for everyone. He beckoned them to the small table in the kitchen so they could eat. Cassidy pulled out her chair and she sat. Without thinking, Cassidy and Deacon both put their hands on either of her thighs. She smiled at how comforting it felt to be sitting there with them, even if she was half naked in a chemise.

Miles looked over his glasses between the three and them, a small smile forming on his lip. "Tate, I take it your day turned out better."

Tatum nodded. "It did. I appreciate everything, guys." Her eyes cut to Deacon, and she tried hard not to blush thinking about his mouth on her just a few minutes before.

"Well," Miles began. "That's good, because you won't have to worry about that Jason anymore."

Tatum put down her fork, confused. "What are you talking about?"

"It means he'll be transferring. I had a talk with Dr. Weatherspoon."

Tatum's eyes widened. "The president of the university?" The thought of the president knowing that she and a student had an altercation was horrifying. She grabbed at her chemise and felt Deacon's hand on top of hers, trying to calm her down. "So, he knows some student tried to fuck me?"

"Obviously I didn't go into great detail," Miles said as he shook his head. "He's a friend, and your privacy is important. All I said was that Mr. Duggar was an unwelcome nuisance for you. Despite his parents being donors, he will be transferring. You won't see him again."

Cassidy chuckled. "I think me paying him a little visit didn't help either."

Tatum's neck swiveled in horror. "Dear God, what the fuck did you do, Cass?"

"Not your concern," Cass squeezed Tatum's thigh. "If it was for you to worry about, I'd tell you." But Tatum stared him down until Cass finally confessed. "Fine. He's alive. Caught him outside the library and had a word. He recognized me from Secrets. Dude just pissed his pants, that's all."

Deacon started laughing but abruptly stopped when Tatum frowned. She didn't know if she should be thankful or angry. "Miles and Cass, you two didn't have to do that. I told you it was fine! I can handle a rowdy student. You act like I haven't been a professor for nearly twenty years."

"I said he's gone." Miles stilled, pushing his glasses up his nose. "I wasn't going to have you in his vicinity anymore. This wasn't up for discussion."

"Miles! Who do you think you are?" Tatum rose from the table, turning toward Deacon. "Deek, thank you for everything. But I think I've lost my appetite."

"Tate," Deacon reached out and held onto her hand. "Darling…please…"

"No." Tatum shook her head, wrestling her hand away from Deacon. "None of you are him! You aren't Frankie! So, stop trying to be." Cassidy stood, but Tatum stopped him, tears welling in her eyes. "I'm going to bed. Please, just let yourselves out."

Tatum walked back up the steps to her bedroom. Angrily, she stripped out of the chemise, tossing it on the floor and climbed under the covers. Tears stained her pillow rapidly. Franklin had been her everything for twenty-two years. Her rock, her hero. Frankie never stepped in to be a savior in situations that she assured him she could handle. Right now, she didn't need any of them to be her savior.

This would not work. Maybe Franklin had it wrong.

Once in bed, Tatum rubbed the space next to her until she fell asleep.

12

THREE TIMES FAST

Tatum placed another scoop of potato salad onto her plate. Nadine's baby shower was lavish, being held at a country club overlooking the river. They decked everything out in various shades of blue to celebrate the coming of little Eddie Junior. They filled tables upon tables with gifts, many of them from Eddie's former teammates and celebrities in attendance. The blue skies against the golf greens were picture perfect. They couldn't ask for a more gorgeous day.

Alisa saddled up next to Tatum in the buffet line, adding a couple of deviled eggs to her plate. She lowered her head to whisper, "I thought I was going to have to call the cops on you. You missed your hair appointment last week. I haven't heard from you in forever! Getting your back blown out by three lucky gents?"

"Shh, Alisa!" Tatum rolled her eyes, moving down the buffet line to the carving station. "You can't whisper worth a damn. And second, I've just been busy with my summer classes, that's all."

"I call bullshit," said Alisa, motioning the server to add salmon to her plate. "I know for a fact summer classes have been over for a week now. By now, we would have been out having margaritas or something. What's up?"

The ladies made their way back to their table where Nadine, Eddie, and Alex were also sitting. She smiled as Eddie rubbed Nadine's stomach gingerly, giving her sweet pecks on her cheek. Alex rolled her eyes at her parents who were clearly annoying her. It was sweet.

"Okay, so spill it, sis," said Alisa, not letting up. "Please tell me you're getting your back blown out."

"Who's getting their back blown out?" asked Nadine, leaning toward the pair. Tatum cut her eyes at Alisa, who winced.

"No one!" said Tatum, throwing her hands up. "Come on, this is a baby shower."

"And a perfect place to talk sex. Given that's how babies are made," chuckled Alisa. Tatum pinched her on her thigh, and she frowned.

"Eddie, can you get me some punch?" asked Nadine, batting her eyes sweetly at her super tall husband.

Eddie laughed. "You ain't slick, Deanie. You just want to get rid of me so you can get this tea. C'mon, Alex, let's leave these chicks so they can gossip."

"Uh huh," protested Alex. "I wanna hear about Auntie Tate and her three boyfriends."

Tatum lowered her head. "I don't have three boyfriends. Eddie, she's exaggerating."

Eddie threw up his hands. "I didn't hear anything. I'm getting punch." Eddie turned with a laugh, grabbed Alex by the arm, and headed toward the punch table. Once the coast was clear, Nadine leaned over as far as her belly would allow. "Tate, what's going on? The arrangement not working out?"

Tatum put some potato salad in her mouth. "I can't say it's doing anything. I don't think this is for me."

"Why? What happened?" asked Alisa, stuffing a meatball into her mouth. "Did things get too freaky?"

"Yeah, but not in the way you would think," said Tatum.

Nadine and Alisa looked at each other, curious. They then stared at Tatum, waiting for some explanation. After watching her pick at a chicken wing,

Nadine put a hand on Tatum's shoulder. "Sis. What-ever it is, you can tell us. We won't judge."

Tatum sighed. "Remember when Alisa and I went to Secrets and we said Cassidy was a cockblocker? What I didn't tell you all was that the young thing he cockblocked ended up being my student."

Nadine audibly gasped while Alisa's jaw was on the floor.

"At first it was okay. I didn't think he recognized me. Then, he came to my office to discuss his grade on a paper and things got really weird."

"Did he hurt you?" asked Alisa, her voice trembling.

Tatum squeezed her cousin's hand reassuringly. "No, girl, nothing like that. He just thought we were playing some kind of game, then tried to come on to me. I told Deacon, who then told Cass and Miles. Miles talked to the university president. Got the poor boy to transfer schools, but not until after Cassidy apparently scared the shit out of him."

Nadine folded her arms over her stomach. "Serves that little shit right! Good for Miles and Cass." Alisa nodded in agreement. "That boy could have blackmailed you for grades or something. I for one am glad Miles flexed his influence to get that boy bounced from the school."

"No! It wasn't their place to do that. I had it

under control. I don't need a savior. I don't need a...."

"Franklin 2.0. Or is it 3.0? I was never good at math," said Alisa with a smirk.

Tatum chuckled. "Exactly. You get my point. I didn't need them to do that."

"So, what *do* you want from them?" asked Alisa. "I think you need to be very clear about your needs. I mean, if you want to continue with this arrangement."

Nadine shrugged as she ate a deviled egg. "Now personally, I think the whole thing is freaky, but you have to tell them what you will and will not tolerate."

Tatum bit her lip. "I know, but...the whole thing was kind of fucking hot."

"Ah! I knew it!" laughed Alisa. "It had you wet, didn't it?"

Tatum blushed, heat rising up her neck. "I can't lie. I was very turned on. Especially after the fact that Deacon ate my pussy until I damn near blacked out just minutes earlier."

"Damn!" said Nadine and Alisa in unison, giving each other high fives. Tatum shook her head, trying to get the two of them to calm down. People were really looking at them.

"Chill, y'all."

"Was it good?" asked Alisa.

Tatum picked up a napkin and fanned. "God, it was so hot. He'd just taken care of me the entire day, you know? Set up a massage at the spa. Cooked for me. Bought me new lingerie. It was so amazing. Maybe because it was things that Frankie would have done for sure."

"Fuck. I'm jealous," said Nadine. "I can't even get Eddie to rub my swollen feet. And he can't even find my pussy. My stomach is enormous!"

All three of the ladies laughed so hard that other tables began looking over at them. Tatum nodded toward their neighbors, sending them sympathetic looks.

"So, any other freaky stuff happen?" asked Alisa. "Sorry, I'm in a drought, so I am living vicariously."

"Well," began Tatum, fidgeting with a cocktail napkin, "I went on a brunch date with Cassidy at Marion's on the River. By the way, he's an astrophysicist. We took a ride on his bike and then went to the planetarium where he…um…finger-fucked me and made me nearly come on his hand."

"Damn, he rubbed your pussy in the planetarium?" said Nadine. "Say that three times fast."

"Wait, he's an astrophysicist!" screamed Alisa. "Oh, Tate, you gotta fuck Neil deGrasse Tyson Beckford now."

Tatum laughed at her friends. "You two are the worst. Seriously, I need advice on what should I do!"

Alisa shrugged. "I don't know, boo. But I think you need to define the rules of this…quadruple…if you want to keep it going."

"Or end it," said Nadine matter-of-factly as she rose from the table. "Let's go find some cupcakes. Little EJ is knocking on my tummy for his sweets fix." Alisa followed Nadine but Tatum waved them off.

"I'm good. I'm stuffed actually."

Tatum pulled out her phone as she watched her best friend waddle around, tugging her cousin along to find cupcakes. They were right. She needed to define the rules of whatever it was she and the guys were doing. She pulled up the group text she'd labeled, "DMC."

TATUM

Can we all talk?

MILES

Absolutely. When?

CASS

Of course, love.

DEACON

What's up?

Tatum slid her phone back into her purse. She wasn't sure what she'd say, but she had four days to get it together.

13

APOLOGIES

Tatum picked Crowne and King to meet the fellas, not only because it was one of the finest steakhouses in the city, but because it was located inside the Griffin Hotel, which had an amazing view of downtown Atlanta. If things went south, at least a spectacular view of the city could console her.

She thought she would meet them there early, but when she arrived, she spotted Miles sitting at a table, scrolling through his phone. She peered at her outfit in the mirror, a simple red tank dress and open toe sandals, and reapplied her matching lipstick before walking toward the table. When she approached, Miles smiled, standing up to kiss her on the cheek.

"You look wonderful, Tate, as always." Miles

155

moved to allow Tatum to sit in their booth. He'd picked a spot closest to the stage where the nightly jazz band would be performing.

"Thanks. I figured I'd get here early but you beat me to it."

Miles smiled. "I got here early to work on what I'd say to you. How to apologize."

Tatum waved her hand. "It's fine. I know you meant no harm in what you did with Jason. It's just that I don't need someone to come rescue me."

Miles took a sip of his bourbon and nodded. "I see. And I guess I need to realize that a lot of women don't need that. I guess I am still operating like I'm dealing with Paula." Miles sighed, looking up at the ceiling before focusing his gaze back on Tatum. "I spent so much of my marriage saving her from something. From the bottle. From the dope. From herself. You aren't Paula. And I'm not Frankie."

Tatum put her hand on top of Miles'. "You aren't. I want to get to know you, Miles. Apart from our ties with Franklin. But now I understand why Franklin felt the need to keep you in my life."

"Why's that?"

"You two are a lot alike," Tatum chuckled. "Quick to take charge. Assertive, but tender toward others. I mean, Frankie wouldn't have gone to the president to get an asshole kid out of my class, but he would have definitely stood up for me."

"Any good man worth his salt would. Especially if they care for you, T. I learned that from Frankie."

A few minutes later, Cass and Deacon strolled in. Deacon carried flowers, and Cass simply carried himself like the fine specimen of man that he was. He wore tight black slacks and a gray fitted polo shirt, his pecs barely contained and his neck tattoo visible.

Deacon handed the bouquet of orchids and roses over to Tatum, who sniffed them with a smile. "I thought I'd bring flowers. I'm not really a flowers kind of guy but, I thought, what the hell?"

Tatum laughed. "Well, I appreciate you making an exception for me."

Cass slid into the U-shaped booth next to Tatum while Deacon was on the other side of Miles. "Hey, Tate." Cass gave Tatum a quick peck on the cheek. She inhaled his familiar leather and woodsy smell.

Tatum smiled. "Hey, Cass. You look great."

He gave her a wide smile, his eyes trailing over her body. "And I can say the same for you. You're wearing the hell out of that red dress, mama." Cass put a hand on her thigh, seeming to settle in for the night.

Miles flagged down the waiter and ordered

drinks. Whiskey and bourbon for the guys and a gin and tonic for Tatum. She wasn't normally a gin girl, but she thought it best to order something a little stronger than her usual martini. She had a feeling she was going to need it.

Tatum took a sip and began. "First, thank you all for coming. I know I've been distant these past weeks, but I needed some time to figure shit out."

Miles nodded. "I can't speak for anyone else, but I missed you."

"Me too," said Deacon.

Cassidy said nothing. He simply squeezed her thigh as his answer. Their responses made Tatum feel warm inside.

Tatum took another sip of her drink. "I appreciate you all stepping up after Frankie asked you all to, but I don't need another Frankie. I need a Cass, Miles, and Deacon. I just want you all to be you."

Cass sighed. "I overstepped with that Jason kid, but I don't like people fucking with those I care about."

Tatum put her hands on Cass' cheek, scratching his beard. "And I appreciate that. In the future, though, I don't want you all to get involved unless I ask." Cass nodded, the glint of his bottom grill flashing before he kissed the inside of Tatum's wrist.

"So, what do you need from us, T?" asked

Deacon, his eyes darting between Tatum and everyone at the table. "I'm all ears."

Tatum finished the last of her gin and tonic, clasping her fingers. "I had a great husband. The best." The table nodded, raising their glasses in acknowledgement. "He made me laugh and smile. I never wanted for anything. I was completely and utterly spoiled. He also knew when to let me fight my own battles. He knew when to step up and when to chill. When Frankie gave you all this oath, I don't think it was about emulating him. It was about being yourselves and giving me the best of you, because he knew that the three of you would care for me in your own way. This is a new chapter in my life. Remember? 'Seasons change.'"

Deacon smiled at Tatum as she recalled his note on her gift.

"And we will," said Miles in agreement. Cassidy and Deacon nodded.

"Good," said Tatum. "Because what I want from you all is simple. We will still date like I said we would. We'll go out. We'll have fun, together and separately. That's all Frankie would have wanted."

"Don't think for a minute that means we still won't step up for you," said Miles. "I'm sorry, but we care for you, babe. We will not let you suffer needlessly. You'll continue to be spoiled and cared for with us."

"Agreed," said Cassidy. "If some shit is foul, we can't stand by. We'll handle it."

Tatum smiled, grateful for this circle of men that Franklin brought into her life. "I know. I appreciate that, but just know that isn't your primary function here."

"Got it," Miles nodded. "Let's just enjoy the night and see where it goes. Next round of drinks on me."

The jazz trio struck up a tune and the foursome eased into relaxed conversation. They laughed about memories and current events. Tatum laughed at Cass telling the fellas about his job, and sure enough, their eyes glazed over. They ordered food and drinks until they were all beyond tipsy.

It was nearing midnight. The jazz band was finishing their set with the very appropriate *Round Midnight*. Tatum wasn't ready to go home, and neither were her fellas.

Her fellas.

She leaned over to Cassidy, her lips grazing the shell of his ear. "I don't want to go home yet."

"Neither do I." Cassidy smiled, his hand slipping

under Tatum's dress until it found her wet panties. She'd been wet for a couple of hours, if she was being honest. Having all three of them there at the same time was sensory overload. He crooked his finger inside, stroking her softly. The moan she let out didn't go unnoticed as Miles and Deacon turned their attention to Tatum.

"Tatum says she doesn't want to go home, yet," said Cassidy. "What should we do for our Tate?" His fingers pumped slowly inside Tatum until she was biting her bottom lip.

"We can get a hotel room," said Deacon. "I'm sure there's a suite available on a weeknight."

Miles stroked Tatum's arm until her skin pebbled with a shiver. "I think we can do that. Tate, what are you thinking? We'll do whatever you want, sweetheart."

Tatum opened her eyes and looked at Miles, Deacon, and Cassidy with a smirk. "Well, maybe tonight we can have some fun. All four of us."

Deacon bit his lip. "Shit, I'm down."

Tatum felt another hand slide into her panties. It was Miles. With the feeling of Miles and Cassidy inside stretching her, bringing her to the brink, she let out tiny gasps, only loud enough for the four of them to hear. She was sure that her sloppy, wet pussy was making obscene noises under the table.

"Would us taking care of you tonight be over-stepping?" asked Miles in a husky voice.

With her bottom lip clenched between her teeth, Tatum could only shake her head to answer that it wouldn't. She couldn't respond or focus. She was coming in the middle of the restaurant.

"I'll take care of the bill," said Deacon, flagging down the waiter. "I can't let you all have all the fun."

When Cassidy hit her G-spot and Miles stroked her clit at the same time, Tatum gripped the table until it shook. "Oh God," Tatum whispered, throwing her head back in the booth. Their booth wasn't exactly private in the restaurant. No doubt patrons around them saw her body react to the men driving her insane under the table.

Miles released his fingers first, licking the wetness off before wiping with a napkin. Cassidy followed suit, licking one finger and placing the other in Tatum's mouth, where she greedily sucked her own arousal off.

Cass smirked, rewarding her actions with a kiss on the lips.

"This should be fun."

SUITE 1007

The suite number was 1007. Tatum took that as a good omen.

It was Frankie's birthday.

The four of them walked into the room, still laughing at some joke that Deacon told on the elevator. But it wasn't all laughs on the ride up to the suite as Deacon took his time to lift Tatum's dress, pull her panties to the side and get on his knees to eat her like a piece of birthday cake. Tatum was sure that they were giving the cameras a show, but she didn't care. She kept her focus on Cass and Miles, who gave encouraging moans between Deacon's loud sucks and slurps. Having an audience just made Tatum wetter and Deacon more thorough with his job.

The suite was luxurious. Floor to ceiling

windows with a gorgeous view of the Atlanta skyline. There was a wet bar and a separate sitting area with a dining room table. The bathroom had a shower that was modern and slick. The bedroom was massive, with a large Cali king size bed that could more than accommodate them.

If it went that far…

Tatum walked to the window to look at the city skyline. Now sober and aware that she was in a hotel room with her husband's three best friends, nerves settled in her stomach. Was she about to do this? She felt hands on her shoulders and looked up to see Miles' reflection in the window. He moved her hair from her shoulder and kissed it lightly.

"We're going at your pace, sweetheart. If all you want to do is sleep, or talk, we will."

Tatum faced him, gently pushing his glasses up on his nose. "I'm fine. I want this. I want you." She looked between their faces. "All of you."

Miles tipped her chin up toward him and lowered his lips onto hers. It took a minute for them to get their rhythm, and when they did, they both moaned into each other's mouths as if they had been waiting a century to kiss. When they broke away from their kiss, Miles grabbed her hand, taking her to the sitting area where Cass and Deacon were in armchairs facing the couch. Miles sat Tatum on the sofa, and without a word, bent down to unbuckle her stiletto heels. He massaged up and down her legs until he rested the ball of her foot on his chin, licking her toes one at a time. Tatum let out a moan, grabbing the sides of the sofa.

While Miles worshipped Tatum's feet, Cass put down his drink and sat next to her. He gripped a fistful of her hair, turning her face toward his. Pressing his lips against hers, he devoured her until his tongue parted her lips. Tatum reacquainted herself with his tongue, enjoying its taste of bourbon and Coke.

"You let Deek taste that pussy and I just got to touch it. Doesn't seem fair, now does it?" whispered Cass as his tongue trailed down Tatum's neck. She shuddered as her senses were overloaded at the feel of Cass' lips on her neck and Miles' tongue between her toes. She opened her eyes to see Deacon still seated in the armchair, watching and palming his dick as he sipped on his whiskey.

"I ate your pussy well, didn't I, darling?" asked Deacon as he stroked his dick through his slacks.

"Open your eyes and answer him," demanded Miles, his lips trailing up and down Tatum's legs.

Tatum nodded, her eyes transfixed on Deacon, who now unbuttoned his shirt.

"Tsk. I need you to use your words, baby girl,"

said Cass, turning Tatum's head toward Deacon. "Tell him how good it was."

"It was so good," moaned Tatum, her pussy growing wetter by the minute. "You felt so good on my pussy, Deek."

Cass smiled against her jawline, then place a soft kiss. "Good girl."

Miles rose from the floor to join Cass and Tatum on the couch. He turned her head toward him, giving her deeper, softer kisses. Tatum made a mental inventory on how each of them touched her, kissed her. Miles was soft and steady, Cass was rougher and demanding, and Deacon was a mix of both.

Miles sucked Tatum's tongue until she was satisfied. "This is your night, Tatum. You are in control, no matter what we say. We do nothing without you, got it?"

Tatum nodded, still breathless from their kiss. "Yes. And do I need a safe word?"

Cass chuckled. "Eventually. For tonight, let's just take it easy."

Tatum smiled. "Okay." She felt reassured that she wouldn't be pushed past her boundaries, but what were her boundaries with three men? She did not know.

"Right now," said Deacon, "We need to get you out that dress. Stand up for us, baby."

Tatum stood. When she did, Cass gave a light smack to her ass which made her head swivel. "I thought you said I wouldn't need a safe word."

Cass looked up through his impossibly long lashes with a smirk. "That was a love tap, mama."

Deacon was now shirtless, his chest chiseled like a statue by Michelangelo. He walked over to Tatum and slowly pulled down the straps of her dress until the entire thing pooled at her feet. Underneath, a strapless red bra barely contained her breasts and her lacy red thong was already wet. Deacon licked his lips. "Perfection, isn't she?"

They all hummed their various levels of approval. Tatum didn't know how sexy and powerful she'd feel by being on display like this. Tonight, three sets of eyes watched her every move. It reminded her of Secrets and all times that she people-watched, getting turned on by the second.

She looked at Deacon, then turned to face Cass and Miles, who were on the sofa, salivating. "I don't want to be the only one here in nothing. Get undressed, please."

Without a word, the men stripped off their clothes. Miles neatly folded his shirt and pants, placing them on the lampstand. Cass stripped off his polo and slacks, haphazardly tossing them on the floor. Deacon took off his remaining slacks, revealing that he didn't have on underwear as his dick sprung free, slapping against his stomach. He was the first man to get naked for her in over twenty years. Her mouth watered, and she wanted to drop to her knees to lick him in appreciation.

Cass wore dark gray boxer briefs, covered with tattoos up and down his torso and arms. Miles wore white boxers, his skin the shade of sepia. The tones of their briefs against their skin highlighted the shape and curve of their dicks. Miles was the thicker of the two, though not by much. Either way, no matter whose dick it was, Tatum realized she'd have to handle them all with two hands and a capable throat.

Tatum eased her backside against Deacon, feeling the length and hardness of his dick at her back while her hands reached into Cass' and Miles' briefs. Cass let out a hiss as Tatum's thumb circled the head; Miles' dick, upon touch, began weeping sticky precum all over Tatum's thumb.

"Is all this for me?" Tatum asked, her stroke steady.

"All of it babe," Cass said hoarsely, his eyes rolling back. "What you going to do with it?"

"I'm not sure, but I like how you feel. Take off your boxers," Tatum demanded.

And they did so, ever so slowly as to tease Tatum. Her chest heaved, and her eyes didn't know where to focus. Three beautiful Black men at her disposal.

Cassidy cupped his balls, giving them a light squeeze as he groaned. His eyes were laser focused on Tatum. "So, what's your pleasure tonight, T?"

Tatum bit her lip. She was nervous but also excited. Horny but also timid. She looked at each man before her, nearly drooling. They all were so gorgeous yet so different.

"Ladies' choice, darling." Deacon's hands moved inside of Tatum's bra, tweaking her nipples between his fingers. She let out a low, hoarse moan, reveling in the electric pleasure that rushed straight to her clit.

Tatum licked her lips, then swallowed before she spoke. "I want Cass to fuck me while Deek and Miles watch."

Miles and Cassidy exchanged a look, then a nod. "I think we can make that happen. Deacon, you willing to watch tonight?"

"Ugh," Deacon let out a playful groan. "If I must. But if Miles is joining me, I know I'll enjoy it." Deacon released Tatum's breasts and gave her a kiss on the shoulder. "You're in good hands, love."

Cassidy took Tatum by the hand, sitting her on the couch. She looked up as he stroked himself to full length and hardness. Without thinking, Tatum moved her hands down to her pussy, fingers dancing between her hot slit. When a bead of precum leaked from Cassidy's dick, Tatum licked her lips. This didn't go unnoticed as Cassidy scooped the liquid bead up with his finger and pressed it against her lips. She licked with reckless abandon.

God, who had she become?

Satisfied, Cassidy removed her fingers. "I'm going to feed you this dick, mama. But not until I get a taste of that pussy. Lean back and spread your legs."

Tatum did as she was told, sitting back on the plush couch and opening her legs until her pussy was hit with a cool rush of air. She felt utterly exposed and brazenly wanton. Frankie would be proud of her.

Cassidy got on his knees before her and lifted her legs higher, up onto his shoulders, forcing her open with a tight hold on her thighs. He licked slowly down her throbbing pussy, moaning when he reached her wet center. He darted his tongue inside, and Tatum nearly bucked off the sofa. This only made Cassidy more focused on driving Tatum insane, moving the rough pad of his tongue up and down her pussy until finally, he latched onto her clit. Deacon may have wanted to satisfy Tatum at the moment, but Cassidy was trying to stake his claim. Her pussy was *his* territory.

Tatum's eyes opened when she felt movement next to her on the sofa. She looked over to see Miles, still in his glasses, looking at her. He held up her hand that she had been touching herself with and licked her fingers.

"Hmm, you taste so good, baby girl. How we feeling?" At that moment, Cassidy sucked her clit with such force that Tatum dug her nails into Miles' thigh. He chuckled. "I take that as, 'we're doing good.'"

Miles continued to pepper Tatum with light kisses as Cassidy sucked and licked her like it was his part-time job. When Cass added two fingers, Tatum felt her body convulse and she squirted her release all over his hand. She moaned into Miles' mouth as she came down from her orgasm.

"Fuck, Cassidy," she breathed out, running her one hand in his hair and another through his beard, now coated with her juices. Cass turned, kissing her wrist. "We aren't done.". He lifted a wobbly Tatum to her feet, holding her by the hand as he headed toward the bedroom. Miles and Deacon weren't far behind.

Once in the room, Cassidy placed Tatum in the middle of the bed. Deacon knelt over Tatum, beckoning her to open her mouth to drink water. "We can't have you passing out when we're just getting started."

Tatum rolled her eyes but drank half the bottle. "I'm not fragile."

"No need to get defensive, darling," smiled Deacon. "This is part of aftercare. Well, in this case, a little in-between care. I'm sure Cass isn't done." They both turned to look at Cassidy, who was now on his knees, lining up his dick with her hot entrance. Deacon kissed Tatum deeply before joining Miles on the settee facing the bed.

"You ready, mama?" asked Cass, his dick inches away from her pussy. Tatum craned her neck to see what was going on around her, but Cassidy's broad shoulders obstructed her view. She wanted to see all of them, all at once.

Cassidy leaned down to lick Tatum's bottom lip. "You'll see soon, mama. But first, I'm gonna fuck you and watch your pretty-ass face when you come on my dick." Before she could answer, Cassidy slowly eased inside Tatum as she grabbed the cloud of pillows surrounding her.

"Fuck, Cass!" She grabbed his muscular ass, pushing him deeper inside her. "Your dick is so big." Tatum wasn't lying. Cass' girth was stretching her to the hilt. Franklin had been a big man too, but Cass was the stuff porn stars were made of.

"Shit…" Cassidy lifted her legs, placing her right leg over his shoulder. "Fuck, Tate, this pussy is so good."

"She's taking that dick so well," said Deacon.

"I bet it's so tight," groaned Miles, who was audibly stroking himself. Tatum wanted to see, but she also wanted Cassidy to keep this pace and fuck her at that angle. His dick was hitting her G-spot with every stroke, sending her into orbit.

Cassidy leaned down, taking a nipple into his mouth between his teeth and gently biting it. As soon as he did that, Tatum felt her body become molten lava as another orgasm rocked her.

"That's it, baby. Come all over my dick," commanded Cassidy, his lips inches from her mouth and they breathed each other in. Tatum's heart felt as if it were racing as fast as a cheetah in her chest. She tried to center herself, but it was impossible. Cassidy was literally fucking her brains out.

"Cass… I…want….to…see…" Tatum squeaked out between Cass' furious strokes.

Without stopping, Cass lifted Tatum like a rag doll, his dick lodged solidly in her, and put her back on her knees to face Miles and Deacon, who were stroking themselves furiously. They were both lean but two different shades of brown, with Deacon being the taller and darker of the two. Their abs glistened with sweat. Miles' fraternity brand on his chest flexed with every tug at his dick. Tatum made a mental note to lick it when she got the opportunity.

"You two are so beautiful," Tatum said as she looked up. Miles gave her a sheepish smile.

"No, Tate, you're the beauty here," said Deacon. "Look at you fucking Cassidy. Taking his big dick. He's so close to coming. Do you want him to come?"

Tatum looked over her shoulder at Cassidy as he thrust into her. Sweat dripped all over his face and chest. When droplets hit her back, Tatum shuddered. She felt a finger stroke her clit, and her chin fell to her chest.

"Oh God, Cass! Fuck!"

Cassidy kept stroking her clit with one hand and held onto her hip with the other. His dick was awakening something deeper and primal inside her.

"Answer them," Cass growled. "Do you want me to come, mama?"

Tatum lifted her head, looking at Deacon and Miles fisting their dicks with precum-covered hands. "Not until they come."

"With pleasure," said Miles.

Tatum watched him spit into his palm, and to

Tatum's surprise, grab Deacon's dick. Deacon let out a hiss as he adjusted to Miles' grip on his dick. Miles leaned over and kissed Deacon, grabbing his face just as Deacon grabbed Miles' length to return the favor. Watching them kiss and jack each other off was too beautiful and too much for Tatum. She felt Cass lift her chin, his firm hand gripping tight. He leaned down to lick the shell of her ear.

"Watch them come for you, baby. You deserve it," he purred, his voice somewhere between a command and a whisper.

Tatum was coming undone watching Miles and Deacon stroke each other. When ropes of thick, white cum hit Miles' stomach, Tatum moaned, digging her toes into the mattress just to get a hold of herself. Within minutes, Deacon followed, spurts of his own nut coating his abs and dripping into his pubic hair. He'd painted his skin like Jackson Pollock, its pattern truly museum-worthy.

Tatum looked back at Cassidy, who clearly wanted to get his. His face was twisted in pleasurable agony, his heavy balls slapped against her pussy, begging for release. "Come, Cass. Come in my pussy," commanded Tatum.

She felt Cassidy's fingers cup her ass, spreading her cheeks until she felt him jerk inside her...once...

twice... Then he let out a sound that was raw and guttural, from the depths of his soul.

Cassidy leaned against her, motionless, trying to catch his breath and jerking each time Tatum's pussy fluttered around his still-hard dick. Cassidy bent down, kissed the middle of her back, and pulled out. "Thank you, baby."

Tatum felt as if she were out of her body. She was someone else, and she hadn't actually felt, done, or seen the things she had. Cassidy leaned against the pillows, semi-hard but softening. She watched Miles and Deacon on the settee, their heavy breathing in sync.

"Come here," Tatum beckoned, purring her request. And without delay, the two of them came closer to her. Tatum sat on her knees at the edge of the bed. She felt Cass' cum spilling out of her pussy. She took two fingers, and massaged her still-throbbing clit with it, giving Cass a show from behind.

"You two aren't clean," Tatum said as more of a question than an observation. She pulled Miles and Deacon close to her, taking both of their dicks in her hands, and began licking them, alternating which taste she'd have in her mouth. She licked their cum-covered fingers and then her own, relishing the taste of sweat and sinfulness.

"Shit," breathed out Deacon, his hands in his massive curls. "Tatum, you're a fucking wonder."

"Clean all this up for us, baby girl," said Miles, who stroked Tatum's wild and loose hair back into place.

Cassidy watched with envy as Tatum licked nearly every drop of cum off their stomachs and dicks. Tatum turned to Cassidy with a wink, extending her hand. "Come join us, Dr. Valentine."

Tatum licked, sucked, and savored each taste of the men until one by one, they were all coming again.

This time, she didn't allow them to waste a single drop.

Tatum woke up to Deacon's arms wrapped around her torso, his soft snores gently purring in her ear. Cassidy was facing her, still sound asleep. She looked over her shoulder to see the top of Miles' head, curled over on Deacon's shoulder. The last time a man was in her bed, it was her son, Morgan.

Now, there were three men in her bed. Three men who clearly didn't want to go. Three men that she wanted to stay there forever.

She wasn't sure what time she went to bed. There

had been aftercare, including water breaks, champagne, berries, and charcuterie from room service between sessions. From bouncing on Deacon's dick while sucking off Miles to having Cassidy finger her until she splashed all over his hands, they had satisfied Tatum in a multitude of ways. They ended the night in the shower, each one of them taking turns bathing her. It all felt like a dream, but Tatum knew this was only the beginning.

Cassidy's eyes fluttered open, and Tatum smiled at him. He was so gorgeous with his round face, full lips, and the fluffiest of beards.

"Hey," she said shyly. "Good morning."

Cassidy leaned over, his beard brushing her nose to place a kiss on Tatum's forehead. "Morning, love. How'd you sleep?"

Tatum smiled. "How do you think I slept? I was nearly boneless and wrung out after last night and this morning."

"That was a teaser." Cassidy gave her a sly grin. "We could have gone longer, I'm sure of it."

Tatum's eyes widened and she let out a giggle. "You all must be a bunch of sex robots or something."

"No," said Deacon groggily. He kissed Tatum's shoulder. "Just men who know what you need and how you need it."

"Right now, I need some pancakes," said Miles as he stretched his long legs, wrapping one over Deacon.

"Y'all want to head over to Pancake Social?" asked Deacon. "I love their breakfast."

Tatum nodded enthusiastically. "Sounds great. It's Friday, so I don't have classes or meetings on campus. I'm down." Cassidy moved a strand of hair from Tatum's face. "I'm down too, but I have work later."

"Stars and constellations?" asked Tatum with a smile. "Will you discover a new planet?"

Cassidy laughed. It was the first time Tatum saw his eyes sparkle. She loved it. "That would be pretty dope."

Miles hopped out of bed first. "Well, Deacon and I have some pretty big cases we are working on. We'll do breakfast and head out." He kissed Deacon's forehead then Tatum's. "Although we'd love to spend the day with you."

Tatum nodded, "I totally understand. I'm not trying to mess up your routine." Tatum wanted to spend as much time as possible with them, but she certainly didn't want to seem like an eager puppy.

Deacon stilled under her touch and Cassidy blew out an annoyed breath.

Miles froze, then sat on the bed. "Tatum, you are

part of our lives now. This isn't just some random thing that we squeeze in between clients and classes, right?"

Tatum sat up, pulling the covers to her neck. "I know. It's just a new normal for me."

"It's going to be a new normal for all of us," said Deacon, still laying on his stomach. "We'll adjust."

Cassidy leaned down and kissed Tatum on her cheek. "C'mon, sweetheart. Get up. Let's go get breakfast and start our day."

Miles held out his hand, encouraging Tatum to follow. "Come on, love."

Tatum smiled, pushing back the covers, and headed toward the bathroom, her fellas following right behind her.

15

INTERLUDE

CASSIDY

After dinner, Tatum had begged Cassidy to take the motorcycle out for a moonlit ride, but he insisted they take his SUV.

Cassidy leaned over and squeezed Tatum's thigh. "I'm glad you like riding, but I got plans for you tonight, mama. And the bike would get in the way." With Cassidy, Tatum quickly learned that it was best to let him do all the planning. And Cassidy never disappointed. From a book talk with Nnedi Okorafor to a movie in the park with a catered picnic, Cassidy knew what Tatum would like and certainly didn't need any help.

Tonight, he told Tatum to dress casually and make sure she brought her reading glasses. Tatum didn't ask why, just slipped on a sundress and sandals and tucked her readers into her bag.

When Cassidy's SUV finally stopped, Tatum realized they were at the Roberts Observatory. She turned to Cassidy and smiled.

"More stars, Captain Planet?" It was a nickname Tatum had begun calling him because she loved to see his face light up like a thousand suns when he talked about his area of expertise.

"You think you know me, huh?" Cassidy pulled Tatum in for a kiss, deeply breathing into her and kissing her with everything. Tatum felt him smile against her lips as it ended.

"Well, we are at the observatory," remarked Tatum.

"True. Tonight, we are going to look at a particular set of stars. They're only visible for a brief period of time this year."

Cassidy quickly opened Tatum's door, pulling her out of the car with ease. Once Tatum smoothed out her dress, they walked up the pebbled walkway to the observatory.

"How much time do you spend here?" asked Tatum, curious to know what Cassidy did and why her husband thought they were a good fit.

"Hell, I'd sleep here if I could. I spend enough time here. "

Tatum looked around. "But they're closed."

Cassidy smiled. "The perks of knowing people. I

did an externship here ages ago. C'mon."

Tatum took Cassidy's hand as he led her to the doors of the observatory. A fresh-faced intern who seemed to swoon over Cassidy and his research met them there. Tatum wasn't sure why, but a twinge of jealousy hit her squarely in the chest.

Get a hold of yourself, she thought.

Somehow sensing her unease, Cassidy held her closer, interrupting the blushing researcher by saying, "I wanted to show my lady what keeps me occupied when I'm not with her."

The young woman looked between them and nodded, her blush fading fast. "Very well, sir. This way." That made Tatum hold onto Cassidy's thick bicep a little tighter.

Tatum was in awe at the telescope seeming to dwarf them.

"This is the largest telescope in the Southeast," whispered Cassidy. "And tonight, we are about to get the clearest view of Sagittarius the entire year."

Tatum turned with a smile. "Wait? Sagittarius? As in, my sign?"

Cassidy winked, putting his hand around her waist. "The one and only."

Cassidy led Tatum up the steps to the telescope. She watched as he plugged in some numbers into what looked like a calculator and the telescope moved. He beckoned her closer.

"Look inside, love," he whispered.

Tatum slipped on her readers and peered inside. She was truly awestruck at the stars, fractals of light that were billions of years away. Cassidy stood close, explaining to Tatum what she was seeing in through the lenses. At every moment, he made sure his hands were on Tatum. Moving a strand of hair from her face. Around her waist. Touching her shoulders, as if he'd done it a million times.

"It makes you realize we are just a fraction of what's out there. It's amazing. The absolute beauty of creation…" Tatum turned to Cassidy, who was staring at her. "Did I say something wrong?"

He shook his head. "No. Not at all. It's funny. When I met you for the first time, I looked at you the same way."

Tatum furrowed her brow, trying to think back on that day nearly ten years ago. Franklin had invited the crew's new basketball partner, Cassidy, over for a dinner party with the rest of their friends. Tatum remembered him being silent and staring. She thought maybe he didn't like her or her cooking. Apparently, that wasn't it at all.

Tatum swallowed. "Really?"

Cassidy nodded. "I know you probably thought I

was being weird, but Frankie always talked about you. How smart you were. How fine you were. Miles and Deacon said he wasn't exaggerating. I thought, 'Yeah, right. Every man thinks their woman is smart and fine.' But then I saw you…and I got it. I lost my senses but had to be cool because Frankie was my boy. So were Miles and Deacon. And I didn't make friends easily. I valued that way more."

Tatum smiled. "He valued your friendship too."

"Yeah, but I sure as hell felt guilty rubbing one out to my best friend's wife."

Tatum let out a laugh that echoed in the vast space. "You can't be serious."

"Oh, yes, I am." Cassidy moved closer, dipping his head down to whisper in her ear. "My dick got hard every time I was near you."

Tatum raised a brow. "Is it hard now?"

Cassidy moved Tatum's hand to the bulge in his pants. "Absolutely."

"I think maybe we need to get out of here."

"Definitely."

They were tearing off each other's clothes before they stepped into the foyer of Tatum's home. Her house was closest from the observatory. The sexual tension that was built up consumed them. They had no time to wait.

Tatum was naked by the time they made it to her steps. She was moving backwards, with Cassidy kissing her furiously. He pressed her down until she sat on the steps.

Cassidy was nearly salivating as he knelt before her. "Let me see that pussy, baby."

Tatum opened her legs wide, revealing a thin, green cotton thong, then slammed her thighs shut. Tatum knew this would drive Cassidy insane. When it was all four of them, they let Tatum dictate the flow of things. Cassidy could work in tandem with Miles and Deacon to get her off.

When they were alone, Cassidy was a different man. He liked to get his way. He liked to be obeyed. And when he wasn't obeyed, Tatum was punished. He was the Jekyll and Hyde of sex, never being one note, and it turned her on.

Scientist by day, dom by night. That was Dr. Cassidy Valentine.

A growl came from deep within Cassidy's throat. "Don't play with me, Tate."

"I'm not playing."

"I'll rip those panties off."

Tatum leaned back on her elbows with a mischievous glint in her eye. "I dare—"

Before she could get the full sentence out, Cassidy ripped off her panties. Tatum moaned, grabbing at his shoulders, but Cassidy held down her wrists with his hands. He looked at her with a devilish gleam in his eyes. She wasn't about to be rewarded until he felt like it.

"I told you to not play with me," Cassidy said as he lifted his head, pushing two fingers insider her slick heat. "When I'm hungry, I expect to be fed." He dove headfirst into her pussy, parting her feverishly hot lower lips with his tongue. When his tongue found her clit, Cassidy sucked with such force that Tatum screamed.

"Fuck Cass!" Tatum yelled as he twisted his fingers to her sweet spot. As soon as Cass found his stroke, she was releasing her wetness all over his hand. Cassidy pulled his fingers out and spanked Tatum's pussy, the zing of the sting sending shocks from her clit to her asshole.

Cassidy rubbed his hands between her wetness, then began stroking his dick with it. "I didn't say come yet, did I?"

Tatum shook her head, so turned on she could barely look at him. "No. But.."

"Uh huh, " Cassidy stopped stroking and squeezed Tatum's pussy, right near the clit. She was going to come if he didn't let her go. "When it's me and you, I tell you when to come. Do you hear me?"

"Yes, Cass."

Cass leaned down, kissing Tatum sweetly. "Good girl."

He lifted her and carried her to the bedroom. Like a pile of laundry, he tossed her on the bed with a bounce.

"Take off the bra, Tate. Let me see those big ass titties."

Tatum did as she was told, taking off her strapless bra and leaning back on the bed. She watched through heavy lids as he stroked himself, getting harder by the second. Every muscle in his abdomen and arms flexed as he touched himself. Tatum was so wet, so turned on. She moved one hand to squeeze her hard nipple and the other to touch her swollen pussy. Before she could take a single stroke, Cassidy was there, swatting her hand away.

"Did I say you could touch yourself?"

Tatum whimpered, fearful that she would cry actual tears. "No. But I can't bear watching you touch yourself without wanting......"

"Then tell me what you want, Mama. Use your words."

"I want you inside me, Cass. Please." With a wet

pussy and agonizingly hard nipples, Tatum was begging for relief.

Cass pulled her legs toward the edge of the bed and spread them like the letter V. He slid into her slowly at first, giving her short, shallow strokes. But Cassidy knew that wasn't enough for Tatum. He sped up, pumping deep into her like a piston as his balls slapped against her pussy.

Tatum could do and say nothing except grip the sheets on her bed. She felt her mouth open but absolutely no sound was coming out, not a peep. She was barreling toward another orgasm and Cassidy knew it. He released one leg and wrapped it around his waist, taking his free hand to grip Tatum's neck firmly.

"You better nut all over this dick, mama.", Cass demanded as his grip tightened, becoming uncomfortable yet arousing.

Tatum was literally seeing stars. Her eyes rolled back, and she felt her back bow slightly off the bed. And she was coming with a fury, creaming all over Cass' dick just like he asked.

Cass barely gave Tatum two seconds to recover when he was flipping her onto her stomach. He slapped her ass once…twice… before biting down on a cheek with his teeth. Tatum winced, the sizzle of pain giving her another hit of endorphins. Before he could ask, Tatum relaxed her face into the mattress, arching her back and ass up.

Cass gave Tatum's ass a playful squeeze. "Look at you, remembering how Daddy likes it." Tatum's pussy muscles tightened, a familiar response. She wouldn't admit it to Cass, but Frankie also said "Daddy" in bed. Maybe he knew that, too. It wouldn't be a surprise.

Cass spread Tatum's ass and spit between her cheeks, pressing a thumb inside her tight asshole slightly. Tatum moaned, adjusting to the intrusion.

"You good, mama?"

"Yes, baby, I'm good," Tatum was panting, in dire need of feeling Cass' dick inside her soon.

As if reading her thoughts, Tatum felt his mushroom head slide inside her pussy. His thumb was still inside her asshole as he adjusted his hips and stance. And for a minute, his movements stilled. God, Tatum loved that part—when Cass' dick was lodged solidly inside her without movement. She felt full, stretched, and satisfied.

Within moments, Cass was moving his dick into Tatum, rocking her hips against his pelvis, and thrusting into her without mercy. His thumb was still in her ass, and he moved his other hand to stroke Tatum's clit. The man was skilled at pulling every single orgasm out of her in multiple ways.

This time, Tatum's orgasm was damn-near violent. She screamed out Cass' name as she nearly pulled him down with her. She felt herself release with a gush that was streaming down her leg and onto the sheets.

"Fuck, Tate!" Cass couldn't hold out anymore. He pulled out of Tatum and positioned his dick right at her asshole and shot his white, hot load like a target hitting a bullseye. Tatum didn't move, relishing in the feeling of Cass' cum dripping down her crack and into her pussy.

"Who would have thought Dr. Simmons was so nasty?" laughed Cass as he fetched a warm washcloth to wipe them off.

Tatum looked over her shoulder, "And who would have thought you were so demanding," she countered.

Cass moved to lie down on the bed. Tatum paused as he moved to Franklin's side the bed. Or what used to be.

"Should I move, baby?" asked Cassidy, concerned with Tatum's puzzled face.

Tatum shook her head, a small smile forming at the corners of her lips. "No, you're right where you need to be."

Cass smiled and pulled Tatum on top of him. He stroked her hair, giving her forehead light kisses. She pressed her head against his chest and listened to the rapid beat of his heart. Tatum realized why Cassidy was not only Frankie's friend, but why Frankie wanted Cassidy to be part of her life. Cassidy was smart, sexy, and spontaneous.

Just like Frankie.

But unlike Frankie, Cassidy was also a risk-taker and thrill seeker—things that Tatum found very attractive. Perhaps Frankie knew Tatum would appreciate those qualities in a partner.

Cass let out a low chuckle. "I know you probably still think this whole thing was crazy. But I don't."

"Not anymore," Tatum said, kissing Cass' tattooed pecs. "Never again."

Tatum needed this.

16

INTERLUDE

MILES

It was only a few weeks before the start of fall semester. Only a few weeks until Morgan came back from his internship. She'd had a rather contentious meeting with the dean about funding for their honor society and postdocs. Dr. Conway argued with her at every step, undermining her authority as department chair. She'd had enough.

When she got back to her office, she checked her phone and Miles had texted to check up on her.

MILES

Hey, baby girl. How's the day going?

TATUM

Rough. These meetings aren't getting easier.

Miles had made reservations at Lotus, a posh Thai restaurant in West Midtown. They talked and Tatum was able to decompress. Tatum chuckled at Miles' neat freak ways as he folded his jacket and unbuttoned his cufflinks, arranging the napkins just so on his lap. Miles told Tatum some joke that Sheila, the longtime receptionist at the firm, had told them and she laughed until she cried. Bottles of wine helped conversation flow with ease, and the stress of the day faded away. It felt natural. Unforced. As if they did this all the time.

Miles convinced Tatum to come to his house for a nightcap. It was a sprawling estate near Alpharetta, complete with a pool and basketball court. Tatum was surprised he hadn't sold it once he divorced Paula. They had had no kids, but knowing Miles, he'd bought that place hoping to fill it with children. The thought made Tatum a little sad, but it explained why he'd doted on Morgan since he was born. There was absolutely nothing he wouldn't do for him. And now, it seems like she could say the same for herself.

After sitting on the sofa sipping a twenty-five-year-old scotch, Miles insisted on running a bath for the two of them. That's where she'd found herself for the past twenty minutes. The Bose sound system throughout Miles' home was amazing. The acoustics in the bathroom made Samara Joy's smooth vocals sound like velvet.

Tatum leaned back against Miles' chest; his long limbs wrapped around her under a mountain of lavender-scented bubbles. Miles focused his attention on washing Tatum's breasts and belly with a loofah in a figure 8 pattern.

"I have a confession," said Miles. "I hope you won't judge me too harshly for it."

Tatum shook her head. "Of course not. You can tell me anything. What is it?"

Miles stilled his hands and let out a deep breath, taking a sip of the rest of his scotch before answering. "I used to really be jealous of Franklin."

Tatum moved her head to look up at Miles. His face was in agony. "Why were you jealous? Frankie loved you. You were his best friend. You built a successful firm together. Shoot, compared to Frankie, you clearly were the more ambitious one. You had nothing to be jealous of."

Miles let out a rough chuckle. "He had everything I wanted. He had you."

Tatum's eyes widened. "Miles... I..."

"Listen, let me explain." Miles took the remote and lowered the volume of the music. "The family. The wife. The love. I thought I could have all of that with Paula. But then it blew up in my face and I had to sit back and watch you and Franklin. Him adoring you. How gorgeous you were pregnant. The home the two of you built was beautiful."

Tears filled Tatum's eyes. She lifted a soapy hand to Miles' cheek, stroking it tenderly. "Our life wasn't perfect, Miles. We had our disagreements and differences. It wasn't always smooth sailing."

"From the outside looking in, it was." Miles shrugged. "If I am being honest, just being around you and Frankie all those years... I fell in love with you ages ago."

Tatum's mouth was agape. "Wow, Miles."

Miles held up a hand, stopping Tatum, whose words were caught in her throat. "I know. You would have never stepped out on Frankie, and I wouldn't have been such a foul-ass dude as to cheat on my wife or hurt my best friend. Doing dirt isn't my thing."

Tatum squeezed Miles' hand. "You're a good dude, Miles."

"Well, I don't know if I am." Miles sucked in a breath, rubbing his forehead, leaving a trail of soap near his brow. "This may sound even fouler to say but when Frankie told us what he wanted us to do, I didn't think twice about it. Didn't hesitate. I knew deep down I was going to say yes because I've loved you from afar for years. Now, with Frankie's blessing, I can love you openly."

Tatum's chest squeezed at his words. She was stunned and moved at Miles' confession, unable to respond. She turned her body in the tub to face Miles and leaned down to kiss him slowly, deeply. Miles grabbed her hips and pulled her down onto his lap, a growing erection making way under the suds. Tatum kissed Miles until her lips were sore and her tongue was electric with tingles.

"Stay with me tonight, baby." Miles breathed the words into her ear. "Please."

"Yes, I'll stay."

Miles led Tatum to his bedroom, not bothering to towel off after getting out the tub. He turned on the fireplace even though it was summer. Tatum looked around the space; it was modern with steely grays and sleek blacks, with a massive black bed in the middle of the room.

Miles sat on the edge of the bed, positioning Tatum in front of him. He kissed down her cleavage to her soft belly. "Your body is so beautiful."

"Thank you." Tatum wanted to cry. Her body had changed so much over the years, and now she was being worshipped. And by three men, no less. Nothing in her life made sense, but she was learning to accept it.

Tatum inhaled a breath, relishing in the feel of Miles' tongue and lips on her body. He lifted her leg onto the bed and dove his tongue between her folds, licking and sucking as if she would quench his thirst. Miles' tongue eventually made its way to her sensitive nub, and he sucked, making her knees buckle.

"Fuck, Miles." Tatum grabbed his head and pushed his face deeper inside her needy pussy. He added a finger to the party, attacking her G-spot until her juices flowed freely on his tongue.

"Your taste… I could bottle it and be a millionaire," Miles said, his breath whispering across her still-wet thighs.

Tatum let out a small chuckle. "You're already a millionaire."

Miles looked up at Tatum, licked her thigh, and smiled. "Fine. Billionaire."

He lifted Tatum up by her ass, eliciting a giggle from her. Laying her down on the cool sheets, Miles kissed her deeply. He sucked her tongue, playfully nipping at her lips. His fingers continued to move inside her, her pussy contracting and squeezing around him.

Miles dipped down, taking a hardened nipple into his mouth. Tatum let out a hiss, arching her back at the dual sensation of his sharp teeth and his fingers.

"Please, fuck me," Tatum panted, near breathless and convinced she could melt into the sheets.

"Whatever you want, sweetheart."

Miles stopped fingering Tatum briefly to reach over into the nightstand for the lube. Tatum watched as he slathered his thick, veiny dick and the smooth head, liquid dripping down to his balls. Even though she was wet, Miles liked it wetter.

Miles eased his slippery dick inside of Tatum, stretching her to capacity. She moaned as she adjusted to him. He pulled her forward, lifting her hips slightly to angle his dick at her sweetest of spots. Tatum cried out, cursing and screaming as Miles rammed into her. Grabbing her legs and pressing her knees into her tits until she couldn't breathe, Miles began moving deeper, circling his hips, and pressing his hands onto her thighs.

"Open your eyes, Tate. Let me see that pretty face of yours come."

Tatum opened her eyes, not realizing she'd closed them, and looked up at Miles, his face the picture of ecstasy and pleasure. Sweat trickled on his brow, down to his chest where that fraternity brand teased her. She lifted her head and licked the shape of the Greek letter, sucking on the end of the brand with a flourish.

"Fuck, Tate!" was all that Miles could say until his body stiffened, and his dick pulsed inside of Tatum, hot and deep. He gently let Tatum's legs down and rested his body on top of hers. Tatum stroked his head, now beaded with sweat. Their still-wet bodies meshed together, remnants of soap suds on the sheets. Miles nipped at Tatum's shoulder, then her ran his tongue along her décolletage. Finally, he looked up at Tatum, a smile on his face.

"Hi," Miles said, resting his chin on Tatum's chest.

Tatum gave a lazy, well-fucked smile. "Hi."

Miles untangled himself from Tatum and went to the bathroom. He came back with a warm towel and parted her lower lips, cleaning every inch of her intimately. The care with which he did so made Tatum realize that Miles' tenderness is what Frankie wanted for her.

"Coming inside you is heaven."

Tatum stroked Miles' head, looking down at him continuing to clean her up. "Feeling your dick inside me is also heaven."

Miles sighed. "Don't judge me. I know it's too late, but getting you pregnant would be a bonus."

"Miles!" Tatum laughed. "There is no way I'd have an infant and a twenty-year-old."

"I know. It's just a fantasy. I will not stop coming inside of you, though. I'm hooked now."

Miles kissed the top of Tatum's pelvis, right near her tiny C-section scar, and tossed the towel in a laundry basket nearest to the bathroom. He eased in bed next to her and pulled the duvet up to cover them. Tatum rested her head on his shoulder.

"Miles? Can I ask you something?"

"Uh-huh," replied Miles, fighting off a yawn. "Anything, love."

"Feeling the way you feel, are you okay with Cassidy and Deacon being involved with me? With us? Tell the truth."

"You know they love you too, right?" Miles sat up on his elbow and smiled. "Baby, my feelings are mine, but you're not mine to claim, and I get it. You are your own woman. And you're ours. Period."

"And Deacon? Given your past with him… Don't you love him, too?"

"I do," Miles sighed. "I've always loved Deacon, and we were always good at the physical with each other. I think timing has always been bad. I was with Paula. He was with…whomever. But…trust me when I say, nothing we've felt compares to being with you. It's as if being with you is like a conduit for our emotions with each other. I mean, we weren't at each other's neck, but we weren't like this either. Being with you has us in a good place. A peaceful place."

Tatum smiled. "That's good to hear."

Miles moved Tatum into the curve of his arm, pulling the duvet over them. He kissed her forehead, brushing away a curl stuck to her sweaty forehead.

"Now, sleep, baby doll."

And they did, listening to the quiet crackle of the fireplace until they dozed off.

17

INTERLUDE

DEACON

Deacon stood behind Tatum, his breath tickling her ear. "You need to relax, darling."

Tatum huffed. "I'm trying, but you're making it hard to focus."

"How?"

At that moment, Tatum could feel Deacon's dick at the small of her back. "You know exactly how. How do you expect me to swing a golf club this way?"

"My bad?" Deacon took a step back with his hands in the air. "You've got it, Tate."

Deacon and Tatum had been at the driving range for a couple of hours. She was terrible at golf, and to be honest, Deacon was no better. He mostly went to the driving range to relax, smoke cigars, and drink.

He insisted they get out, get some fresh air, and soak up some sunshine because they couldn't spend all their free time in bed. Tatum objected to that idea greatly, but Deacon wouldn't budge. He had an entire day planned for them and he didn't want to waste it.

Over the past few weeks, Tatum realized Deacon liked to keep himself busy. Even with work as a forensic auditor for the firm, he worked on a ridiculous amount of cases at once. He enjoyed keeping the plates juggling. That explained a lot, especially with his dating history. Frankie used to joke and call him "Dick-em-Down-Deek." Love them, leave them, and add another to the rotation.

Tatum took a swing, her ball barely going anywhere. "D, this is ridiculous. I suck at this."

Deacon took a sip of his beer and laughed. "You're so tight. You need to relax. Open your stance. Follow through with the swing."

Stance? Swing? It all sounded Greek to Tatum as she leaned against her club. "I can't do this."

Deacon took a long puff of his cigar. Tatum didn't like smokers, but Deacon smoking a cigar was very sexy. "Do you need me to eat your pussy out here in the open to help you relax?"

The thought made Tatum shiver. They would for sure give these good ol' boys a show. Tatum stared at

Deacon as he sat there, long legs spread wide in his khaki shorts. The look on his face was one of utter seriousness. Tatum swallowed, then let out a nervous laugh. "You aren't serious. C'mon now."

"As a heart attack, baby. I don't care if people watch me. Neither should you. Your pussy is something that deserves to be shown off. Which reminds me, the second part of our date. You ready for it?"

Tatum rolled her eyes, adjusting her ball cap. "I would be if you told me what it was."

Deacon laughed as he put out the end of his cigar. "It's a surprise, darling. What fun would it be if I told you?"

Tatum walked over, sitting on Deacon's lap. She purposely ground her ass into his crotch. "Even if I begged a little."

"Oh, doll," Deacon groaned, his lips finding the curve of Tatum's neck. "Not gonna work on me. I have willpower." Willpower or not, Tatum knew Deacon couldn't ignore the growing hard-on in his slacks.

"You don't play fair, Tate. You want me to nut in my pants?"

She pressed her ass down further until Deacon let out a moan. "I don't play at all. Tell me what's the surprise, babe."

Tatum felt Deacon's hand breach the top of her

golf slacks, making its way inside and settling on her mound. His long fingers parted her lips and rubbed her until she was wet and slick. "Come first and I'll tell you, love."

Tatum let out a moan so loud she was sure that others heard her. Her teeth dug into her bottom lip as she tried to stifle her rising orgasm, but it was useless. Deacon had her number and was dialing it with his fingers.

Tatum dropped her head, her cap nearly coming off. "Oh God, shit!" She dug her nails into his thighs, trying to hold on to brace herself for the next orgasm.

But Deacon stopped, pulling his hands out of her pants. "Looks like I win."

Tatum turned to face him, watching as he licked her off his fingers. "You're a jerk."

Deacon smirked. "That I am."

Deacon pulled his Audi R8 into a warehouse area off of Arizona Avenue near Edgewood. If Tatum was with anyone else, she'd be more than afraid that she'd be tomorrow's news headline.

Deacon put a hand on her knee. "Don't worry, babe. I am not trying to wrap you in plastic."

"I'm not so sure about that." Tatum looked out of the window. "Where the hell are we?"

"My little piece of heaven. I'll show you."

Deacon exited and opened Tatum's door, helping her out of the low-profile car. He put in the code to the building and opened the door. When Tatum walked in, she was surprised. It was a fully furnished loft but with massive photos on the walls. Some of nude and semi-nude men. Some of the city skyline at various times of the day. Some were fully in colors while others were in black and white.

Tatum looked around in awe. "Gorgeous photos. Wait… I thought you lived in John's Creek."

Deacon brought Tatum over a **glass** of wine. "I do. This is my photography studio. I shot all these photos on the wall."

"Seriously?" Tatum moved closer to look at a photo of a pregnant woman, only covered in gauze. "Why didn't I know this?"

Deacon shrugged. "It's not something I really told a lot of folks about."

"So why aren't you doing photography full time? Clearly, you have a gift."

"I take a job here and there." Deacon took a sip of wine, tapping the glass. "My parents were just two blue collar folks, working in a chicken plant. They wanted me to make money. So, I picked the safe major. I went to law school. Became a CPA.”

“It’s not too late, Deek,” smiled Tatum. “I say you go for it.”

“Really? I’d have to talk to Miles about it.” Deacon motioned for them to sit on the couch. “I helped a lot with the firm. And with Frankie being gone…”

Tatum put a hand on Deacon’s leg. “Please don’t use Frankie’s death to be an excuse to not live your dream.”

Deacon intertwined his fingers with hers and lifted them to his lips. “What about you, Tate? Dreams? What do you want now that Frankie is gone?”

“That’s tough.” Tatum let out a sigh, thinking about the last twenty-two years. “I don’t know. Just to be happy. I’ve already done a lot with Frankie.”

Deacon twirled his fingers through Tatum’s messy ponytail. “Did you ever think happiness would include me, Miles, and Cassidy?”

“Hell no!” Tatum let out a laugh that echoed throughout the loft. “Absolutely not. But now I understand why Frankie asked you all to do this. You really are the best men for me.”

Deacon leaned in and kissed Tatum, softly and sweetly. He pulled her hair loose from her ponytail and ran his fingers through it. Tatum’s hands found their way underneath Deacon's shirt where her nails grazed his abs. He let out a low moan into her mouth, finding her tongue to suck on.

"Tell me," whispered Tatum. "What's the surprise?"

Deacon smiled against Tatum's lips. "The photos. I want to photograph you. Naked."

Tatum pulled back. "Seriously? Deek? Naked?"

"Yes, darling." Deacon began unbuttoning the top of Tatum's polo, still kissing her at the hollow of her throat. "Naked. I want to see everything."

Tatum felt her heart beating faster. She thought about every stretch mark, every bit of cellulite, her C-section scar, her sagging breasts. Deacon placed a hand over her heart.

"Don't be nervous, Tate. You're in expert hands. Always."

Tatum nodded. "Okay."

In total silence, Deacon undressed Tatum. Their breathing was the only sound in the room. Pulling her polo above her head and unfastening her bra within seconds, Deacon lifted each breast, circling around a nipple before sucking hard. Tatum leaned back, relishing the feel of the pressure of Deacon's tongue. His hands moved down, unbuttoning her golf slack. Tatum lifted her hips as Deacon pulled them down, along with her panties, into a pile at her feet. After removing her socks, he helped her step out of them and led her to the back.

The second room in the loft was Deacon's studio. The exposed brick walls were plastered full of Deacon's photographs. Full of backdrops, chairs, blankets, and tripods, he had all the equipment necessary for a shoot. Light boxes were set up, and the backdrop was simply white with a black stool. The camera was already positioned on an adjacent table.

"You ready, darling?"

"Y-yes," Tatum stuttered, nervously looking down at her feet. She felt so exposed and raw.

Deacon lifted her chin., placing the softest of kisses on her lips. "These pics are for us. Miles, Cassidy, me, and you. No one else, okay?

Tatum nodded. "Alright."

"Here," Deacon wrapped a silk robe around her shoulders. "Get comfortable. Sit on the stool while I check the lighting."

In no time, Deacon set up the lighting and turned on some music. He also removed his shirt. He stood there in only his khaki shorts, somewhere along the way taking off his socks and shoes. Tatum stared at Deacon as he inspected his camera lens. The hard lines of his body were on full display, wrapped in a deep chocolate package that one could only call "blessed." Tatum's eyes lingered on the V shape that dipped into his shorts. She'd always loved that part on a man, especially if it was well-defined.

"Like what you see?" asked Deacon with a smirk as he adjusted his lens.

Tatum licked her lips, not caring that he caught her. "I do."

Deacon looked through his viewfinder. "I do too. Now, take off the robe."

Tatum eased out of the silk robe, tossing it to the side of the stool. Her nipples hardened as they hit the cool air. Deacon leaned back, looking at Tatum with a cocked head.

"What?" Tatum asked.

Deacon said nothing. He came over to Tatum and opened her legs, wide., positioning one up higher than the other on the stool. "Now, put your hand down there and throw your head back."

Tatum did as she was told, feeling totally exposed, but equally turned on. Her nipples were hard and her pussy thrummed. Her nerves were still there but slowly being replaced by arousal and excitement.

The shutter began clicking rapidly as Deacon moved around her. Between shots, he repositioned her. He sprayed oil on her body. He draped the sheer material over her frame. He kissed her, reassuring her how amazing she looked. He shouted out things for her to focus on or think about. Last, he gave her a sleek black dildo. It was a little longer than Deacon, but just as thick. Tatum raised a brow.

"What do you want me to do with this?"

"Inside you," Deacon looked up from his camera. "Slide it inside you. Are you wet enough?"

Not exactly, but Tatum was getting there. She rubbed the dildo up and down her slit, coating it with the juices that were forming. She heard the shutter click rapidly. Tatum had done nothing like this before. She trusted Deacon. When she finally plunged the dildo inside of her, she heard Deacon moan.

"Move it inside you, Tate. Imagine it's my dick, darling. Me making you feel so good."

Tatum did as she was told as the noises from her pussy could be heard intermingled with the music. Tatum opened her eyes to see Deacon on his knees, his camera pointed straight at her weeping, wet pussy.

Deacon licked his lips, his camera still aimed squarely on the subject. "God, you look delicious. Are you going to come for me? Please, darling. Come for me."

Tatum was close, so close that she nearly rocked herself off the stool. She caught herself, holding on with one hand while the other pumped deeper inside, her pussy making squelching noises and pulsating around the dildo. When she was about to come, she threw her head back and yelled something incoherent. She could hear nothing but the sound of shutters as she climaxed.

When she'd come down from her orgasm, Deacon retrieved the dildo and handed Tatum a bottle of water. After helping her off the stool and onto the plush futon, he gave Tatum several reassuring kisses before putting the robe back around her shoulders. "You couldn't take a bad shot if you tried, darling."

"Is this really me?" It amazed Tatum looking at the shots on the small LCD screen on the camera. The photos of her mid orgasm were intense, and somewhat beautiful in their ability to show her in a new way—raw and uninhibited. Free. The photos of her pussy were less anatomical and more *Penthouse*. Very high art for something so sexually charged.

Deacon looked up from the camera. "Of course it is. I can't fake this kind of beauty. Naked or not, you haven't changed since the moment I met you."

Tatum felt her body warm all over. "Seriously? That was nearly twenty years ago."

"I remember when I first saw you," Deacon resumed, taking photos as he spoke. "Standing by the window at the NCCU Law School L1 event. Looking sad."

Tatum smiled, remembering it fondly. "Yeah. My so-called date ditched me, and I was just standing there babysitting a Coke. It was the night I met Frankie."

"Actually, I'd seen you first." Deacon confessed. "You were so gorgeous in that orange dress."

Tatum's eyes grew wide. "You remember what I had on?"

"Of course. I thought to myself, that girl in the orange looks so juicy. I was about to go up and talk to you when I got pulled away for a second. Then Frankie came up to me and said, "I just met my wife." He didn't have to tell me it was you. I knew. Then about fifteen minutes later, Miles said, "So, I just saw this girl..." You had that thing about you, you know?"

Tatum smiled. "Yeah, that's what Frankie said."

Deacon leaned against his desk. "I never told him that night I had the same thought. He just beat me to it."

Tatum let out a laugh, but Deacon didn't join her. "Oh, you were serious?"

"What's so funny? Never thought of me as the marrying kind?"

Tatum shrugged. "No. You just never settled down. Never even talked about it."

Deacon shook his head. "Why would I? When my best friend already had the best girl in the world?"

Tatum frowned. "But there was Miles…"

Deacon gave Tatum a sly smile. "Miles and I are best the way we are. Physically, professionally, we're great. But I think we both were too into you to be in love with each other."

Tatum got off the futon and stood in front of Deacon. "Stop it, Deek." She drug her nails across his chest. Deacon dropped his head back, groaning deeply.

"It's true. You have no fucking idea how amazing you are."

Deacon kissed Tatum, wrapping his arms around her and lifting her off her feet and onto the desk. "I'm tired of staring at you naked. And I'm tired of talking. I'm trying to fuck you." Deacon moved Tatum's hand to the crotch of his shorts where his dick was hard already. "I've been hard the entire time I've been taking pics."

"Then let me take care of it."

Tatum was already unbuttoning Deacon's shorts before she got an answer. His dick sprung free, slapping against his stomach before settling into a steady bob. Deacon was so tall that Tatum didn't have to bend down or up very high to let her mouth settle onto his dick. She cupped his balls and slurped the drizzle of precum down, savoring the taste of him. Since she began fucking them, Tatum had learned to recognize all three of the guys' taste and essence. By far, Deacon's was her favorite flavor of them all. Tatum eased into a steady rhythm, sucking, slurping, and moving up and down Deacon's shaft with ease.

Deacon grabbed a fistful of Tatum's hair before driving his dick deeper down her throat. When her eyes watered and she gagged, he let her go so she could catch her breath, only to do it all over again seconds later.

Deacon took a thumb and wiped the tears from Tatum's cheek. "Look at my pretty princess with my dick deep in her throat. I know you can go deeper. Can't you, darling?"

When she didn't think she could, Tatum's mouth opened wider, spit mixed with precum pooling in the corners and dribbling down her chest and onto her robe. Loving the mess she was making, Deacon pushed the robe off Tatum's shoulders, leaving her fully exposed, on her knees, and nearly breathless. Deacon's dick hit Tatum's uvula, and breathing through her nose was all she could do to not get lightheaded. Tatum tapped his arm, their signal for when it was becoming too much. When Deacon pulled out, Tatum coughed, grateful for the air but missing the taste and feel of him already.

Deacon swiped something from the desk and took Tatum's hand, moving them to the center of the room. He picked her up, curling her thighs on his biceps, and slowly lowered her onto his wet, hard dick. Tatum let out a deep, throaty moan. She was getting all dick from Deacon, hitting her deeper than ever.

"Hold onto me, darling," Deacon grunted as Tatum wrapped her arms around his neck. He bounced her on his dick, and every few seconds, a flash would go off. Tatum realized that Deacon had picked up a remote to control the camera and was taking pictures of him, dick-deep inside Tatum.

Deacon kept hitting her spot and in response, she clawed his back and made a mess all over his dick. The curve of Deacon's dick was ringing her G-spot like a doorbell.

Tatum panted, hair stuck to her face. "Deek, Fuck! I can't hold on."

"Yes the fuck you can, darling."

Tatum's admission only made Deacon go harder and faster than before, until Tatum had gone limp in his arms from the orgasms. And with the last few pumps, Deacon was spilling inside Tatum with reckless abandon.

Deacon pulled out of her and carried her to the futon. He massaged her legs, kissing her calf muscles that were deliciously sore from the position. Tatum loved how he never skipped a moment to cherish her, to touch her as if she were a delicate flower.

"Are we done?" asked Tatum, looking down at Deacon. He was drenched with sweat, yet his dick was still hard. It was a marvel that the man seemed to recover so fast.

He pulled her by the legs, closing the gap between them, and got on his knees, readying himself to dive into her pussy.

"I'll never be done with you."

18

A NEW NORMAL

*T*atum rocked her newest godson in her arms. "Nadine, EJ is the most gorgeous baby I've ever seen. Next to Morgan."

"And Alex," chimed in Nadine as she watched Tatum on the sofa. "She was literally a baby model!"

Tatum sniffed the top of his head, getting a hit of instant dopamine. She smiled, thinking of Miles and how he'd love to have a baby with her.

"And what's got you smiling? Because I know it isn't EJ. I am pretty sure he just took a stinky poop!" said Nadine with a quizzical look as she reached for EJ.

Tatum shrugged. "It's nothing. Just thinking about something Miles said."

"Ooh, Miles!" mocked Alisa as she sipped her sangria. "No wonder we haven't seen you in weeks. You haven't even been by the shop for me to touch up those roots. So, how's it going with your boyfriend? I mean, boyfriends."

Tatum pursed her lips. "Do you really want to know, or do you want to judge me?"

"Well, I can't make any promises," Alisa laughed.

"I love you, but I admit, I am judging," said Nadine, who was feeding EJ with one hand and balancing a plate of pasta on the other. A true Superwoman.

"I thought this was insane at first," Tatum said as she leaned back, biting her bottom lip. "But now it makes sense. Each one of them has qualities I enjoy. Miles is sophisticated. We do the art shows, wine tastings. When I can't sleep, he's a phone call away. Deacon is funny and sweet, flirty and creative. And, well, Cassidy…"

"Is bending you like a pretzel!" interrupted Alisa. Her response made Nadine cackle and give her a high five.

Tatum rolled her eyes. "If you must know, yes, the sex is phenomenal. He's aggressive, command- ing, but he's also really brilliant. If something is broken, he fixes it. My gas tank is always full because he fills it. He reads NK Jemisin with me, for God's sake."

Tatum looked at her friends who said nothing.

Alisa was wide-eyed, and Nadine simply stared, rocking EJ in her arms. "What is it? What did I say?"

"So, you built-a-boyfriend from three men? Damn, I can't even get one dude to call me back!" Alisa groaned, folding her arms.

"I think it's kind of brilliant," said Nadine, to which Tatum and Alisa turned in surprise. "What? I mean, no man can be everything to you. No matter how much you love them. Shoot, sometimes I wish I had an extra husband who did the things I know Eddie wouldn't. And with you losing Franklin, there is no one that can truly take his place. But he knew the right men for the job."

"That's all well and good," said Alisa, chugging the last of her Sangria. "Tell me about the dick! How is it? Do you sleep with each of them or all at once?"

"Yes," said Tatum.

"Yes, what?"

"Yes to both."

Alisa and Nadine squealed, nearly waking up the peaceful EJ. Nadine signaled for the nanny to put EJ in his crib so she could properly gossip. "Bitch, we need details."

Tatum shook her head. "I don't want to go there. Just know that I am well satisfied."

"All three of your holes are getting work, huh?" asked Alisa.

Tatum took a sip of her sangria and said nothing.

"There's your answer, Lisa!" laughed Nadine. "Our girl reached her mid-forties and finally became a slut."

Alisa smacked Nadine on the arm. "Nadine, slut-shaming is so 2000s. Tate is allowed to get her freak on. We are in the prime of our lives. I am proud of her."

"Exactly," said Tatum. "Frankie and I had so much more life ahead of us. So many things we wanted to do. Including in the bedroom. Now, I get to live out my fantasies. I mean, granted, I had a good time in college, but not this good."

"But are you happy?" asked Nadine.

Tatum thought about these past few weeks. How nervousness and hesitation had been replaced by excitement and joy. Joy she hadn't felt in forever. "Yeah, I am. Truly."

Alisa raised her glass. "Well, cheers to that because that is all that matters!" All three of the ladies clinked their glasses in salute.

Tatum's calendar alarm buzzed. Confused, Tatum slipped the phone out of her pocket and stared. Her heart slammed against her ribcage.

"What is it, Tate?" asked Alisa.

"Just a reminder that what would have been our twenty-third anniversary is in two weeks."

"Oh, Tate," Nadine reached out for her friend's hand, clasping it tight.

Tatum squeezed her eyes shut, trying not to let the tears crash down. "It's fine, really."

"You need to take your mind off that day," said Alisa, handing Tatum a napkin. "Maybe we can go out for the day? Get a massage or something. Or maybe you call your new boos and celebrate Frankie."

Tatum dabbed the tears away from her face. "Celebrate with them? You don't think that's a little strange."

Nadine guffawed. "Please. No stranger than this arrangement y'all got going on."

Alisa gave Tatum a squeeze on her shoulder. "Get that back blown out in honor of my boy Frankie."

Tatum looked at her cousin and squinted, then burst out laughing. "I can't stand you."

Alisa kissed Tatum all over her face, much to her chagrin. "You love me, and you know it!"

19

ANNIVERSARY

*I*n the days leading up to what would have been her twenty-third anniversary with Frankie, Tatum was less tense. Tatum realized Frankie wouldn't want her to be sad, wallowing in her misery. Instead, she refocused her energies on preparations for the fall semester and Morgan's arrival from his internship in DC. It was all she could do to keep herself from crying her eyes out.

Alisa and Nadine suggested a hot yoga class that morning. Tatum agreed, hoping that it would help her relax and bring good energies for the day. As she stretched and sweated, Tatum thanked God for the years she got to spend with Frankie and hoped that he was in a better place, celebrating their love.

When Tatum returned home from an impromptu brunch after yoga, she was met with a giant bouquet on her kitchen island and a gold box next to it. Clearly, one of the guys had dropped it off while she wasn't home. Tatum picked up the note on the flowers and read.

Tatum clutched the note to her chest and exhaled. They really were the most thoughtful group of men in the world. She was extremely lucky to have them in her life. Tatum put down the note and picked up the box. It had some weight to it. Was it jewelry? She wasn't sure. Tatum pulled the ribbon and opened the top of the box. She gasped. It was jewelry alright—a 24k gold anal plug with a diamond center. This had to have been Deacon. Deacon loved toys. There was another note underneath.

"This is for tonight. Wear it when we pick you up at 8."

No sooner had she read the note that her cell phone rang. She smiled at the avatar on the screen. It was Miles.

"Hey Miles," Tatum said. "Am I to assume you were the one at my house this morning?"

Miles' full-bodied baritone laugh made Tatum

smile. "Actually, no. It was Cassidy. But the box is from Deacon."

Tatum laughed. "I figured that much. Where are we going at 8?"

"It's somewhere that we can all be together. Without judgment. "

Tatum swallowed. There was only one place like that. "Secrets? Are you serious?"

"Yes."

"Are you all sure you want to?" Tatum scratched her head. She thought about the last time she was there and ran into her student. Dear God, she couldn't get into another situation like that again.

"Yes. Tonight is about your pleasure, Tate. Tonight, we're completely yours. Be ready at 8. No worries, we'll take all measures to be discreet. I've arranged for a car service to take us there from your place."

Tatum twirled her wedding band. Secrets? With them? Yes, she and Frankie had gone a time or two for their anniversaries, but she never in a million years would have imagined going as the center of a quadruple. Hell, she hadn't imagined a life without Franklin at all. Yet, as the summer was drawing to a close, Tatum's heart had grown to make space for the three of them in a new and profound way.

It wasn't love. Not yet anyway. But with every

intimate encounter and intimate interaction, sexual or not, Tatum realized that her feelings for Miles, Deacon, and Cassidy went beyond friendship. It was a dynamic that straddled the line between deep commitment and devotion.

After her shower, it took Tatum about thirty minutes to settle on a satin green slip dress with strapless lace green underwear underneath. Green had been Frankie's favorite color. Tatum wore her hair bone straight with a severe middle part caressing the top of her shoulders, completing the femme fatale look with blood red lipstick and a spritz of her signature Tom Ford perfume.

She opened the door to meet Miles, who had arrived first. He wore a simple black button down and black slacks. A wave of heat engulfed her body as his eyes traveled all over her body, finally landing on her lips.

Miles leaned in for a kiss at the corner of her lips. "God, Tatum. You look fucking amazing. I don't want to mess up your lipstick."

Tatum smoothed out his linen shirt. "I can always reapply." Truth of the matter was, she wanted to kiss him, too.

"Nah, I know how women are with makeup. I have all night to get those lips messed up."

Deacon and Cassidy arrived almost at the

same time, with Cassidy pulling up on his bike. Deacon's curls were shorter today, pulled together with his simple tan polo and slacks. He looked very business casual. Cassidy wore boots, ripped jeans, and the tightest gray t-shirt that seemed poured over his pecs. The three of them together looked like a spread in GQ. Tatum was salivating.

Deacon took a few strides with his long legs and kissed Tatum on her cheek. "You look delicious, darling. Doesn't she look good, Cass?"

Cass said nothing. He simply stepped to Tatum and pulled her in for a kiss, palming her ass. Clearly, he didn't get the memo about lipstick, which made Tatum chuckle against his lips. When they pulled back, Miles rolled his eyes while Deacon shook his head.

"What?" asked Cassidy, looking at the two of them. "I can't kiss my girl?"

They both threw up their hands laughing.

Tatum grabbed her shoes—a pair of gold lace-up stilettos. "Which one of you is going to help me with these?"

"That would be me," said Deacon, and he knelt down to place Tatum's foot inside the sandal and tie them up. He did so with such intricacy that Tatum feared she'd never get them off. She wondered how good he was with ropes and if there would be any tonight. She certainly wouldn't mind.

"And what about the gift?" asked Cassidy. "Do you have it on right now?"

Tatum almost forgot. "Shit. I have it in my purse, but I haven't put it in yet. I was going to wait until we got there."

Cassidy took her hand and led her upstairs before she knew it. She heard Miles say, "Well, damn," as he and Deacon began chuckling.

Once in her master bathroom, Cassidy held out his hand. "Let me have it, Tate."

Tatum looked in her purse and handed him the gilded object. "I mean, I could have done it myself."

Cassidy looked up with a glint in his eye. "What's the fun in that? Let Daddy handle it for you."

Tatum swallowed, more than turned on. "Fine. Just be gentle."

"Aren't I always gentle?"

"Ha," Tatum laughed. "You? Gentle?"

Cassidy huffed. "You might be right. Where's the lube?"

Tatum pointed to a drawer in her bathroom and Cassidy opened it. She watched as he slathered an ample amount of lube onto the plug.

"Pull your dress up and bend over the counter."

Tatum slowly lifted her dress and pulled her

panties down. Behind her, she heard Cassidy let out a low growl as he came behind her. She felt the cool, wet object at the opening of her ass as she gripped the counter.

"Relax, mama. I got it."

She felt Cassidy's other hand stroke her clit as he slowly pushed in the anal plug. Tatum shouldn't have been ready to come, but she was. When Cassidy tried to move his hands, she grabbed him.

"Don't stop, please," she begged as she looked at him standing behind her in her mirror.

Cassidy gave a smirk and squeezed her pussy in his hands. "Not yet. We have plenty of time for that. I just wanted to relax you to get that in. And it seems like it worked." He kissed her shoulder sweetly. "How do you feel?"

Tatum stood up, adjusting to the intrusion. "God, I feel full."

"You ain't felt full yet." Cassidy promised. "Let's go."

Promptly at 8 p.m., a blacked-out SUV picked them up to take them to Secrets. The ride over was fairly silent. Tatum was nervous, but she shouldn't have been. She couldn't have been in better hands with the three of them. Each time the SUV hit a bump or turn, she felt the plug inside her and had to bite her lip to focus on the feeling of arousal permeating inside her.

"I bet it looks so good back there," whispered Deacon loud enough for only the four of them to hear.

"It does," remarked Cassidy. "You have good taste."

"Thanks. Only the best for our girl."

"Always," said Miles as he placed a hand on Tatum's thigh, moving up slowly. "The best is what she deserves."

Tatum smiled, not saying a word. Suddenly, she felt the anal plug vibrate. She grabbed the side of her seat and let out a low moan.

"By the way," Deacon said with a smirk, "I forgot to mention there's a little surprise."

"I love surprises," said Miles. "Can the surprise go higher?"

With that, the buzzing intensified, and Tatum nearly screamed. "Could you please...oh God... please..." Tatum hoarsely begged. She prayed their driver did not know what was going on.

"Please what?" asked Cassidy. "What have we told you about using your words?

Deacon chuckled. "Yes. Use all those words, Professor."

When the buzzing subsided, Tatum let out a

chuckle. "I can't stand you all." And with that, the tension and nervousness were gone, replaced with a sexy playfulness that was certainly reminiscent of times with Frankie.

The limo slowed down, and the chauffeur opened the doors to the SUV. The main concierge, who was holding a tablet in hand, greeted the group.

"Welcome back, Mr. Valentine. We've taken great steps to ensure a pleasurable experience for you and your guests. Follow me this way for your private room."

After the group signed the standard waivers, the tuxedo-clad concierge at Secrets stepped around the counter and beckoned the group to follow him through the velvet curtains. Instead of going into the main area with the dance floor and buffet, they made a swift left past the bar to a private set of steps leading downstairs to a dimly-lit corridor. Tatum had never been down here before, but she'd heard stories. Frankie had put it on their bucket list of things to do. Looked like she was crossing it off her list tonight.

The concierge stopped in front of a room, opening it with a keycard. It was a red-lit room with a massive four-post bed in the middle and benches along two of the walls, the others being massive mirrors. Four masks in varying styles were on the bench. Various floggers, feathers, gags, and cuffs hung on the walls. In another corner was a large, black St. Andrew's cross with a bench attached. Tatum almost didn't see the masked bartender who was already mixing mocktails, as they permitted no alcohol in the play area. He was shirtless and had locs. Immediately, Tatum knew it was the handsome bartender from the last time she was there. The thought of him seeing this made her feel a warm rush up her spine.

"Welcome to the Premier Suite of the Dungeon at Secrets." The concierge handed Cassidy the keycard as he began gesturing around the room. "As you can see, we've taken care of everything for you. You do not need to leave. Mr. Valentine already sent over beverage and food orders, which will be taken care of. All drinks must be non-alcoholic. We also do not permit any illicit drug use. There is a private bathroom with lubes, lotions, and condoms, and a full rain shower that can accommodate a party of your size comfortably. Mr. Valentine has selected several toys for your enjoyment. There is no smoking in the room, but wax play is permissible. If you need anything, page our staff. Enjoy."

Tatum walked up to the mirror, putting her hands on the glass. She couldn't see anyone but she knew that there was someone on the other side of the mirror.

"It's two-way glass." Miles came behind her, wrapping his hand around her waist and placing a wet kiss on her bare shoulder. "They can see us, but no one will know who we are, love. I know you love to watch, but this time, they'll watch you."

Tatum turned, wide-eyed at Miles. "How did you…" She didn't bother to finish asking. She knew how he knew. Franklin. There truly had been no secrets between brothers, it seemed.

Cassidy brought Tatum over a club soda with lime. Deacon joined them, handing Miles a Coke. They all raised their glasses and clinked them before taking a sip.

"Tonight is all about your pleasure, T," said Miles, taking Tatum's hand. "So, you establish the pace. And the safe words. What are they?"

Tatum swirled her glass around before thinking. "I don't want to rush anything. I think Green, yellow, and red are just fine." When she and Franklin did light sub/dom scenes, those always worked for them.

They all nodded in agreement. "If anything is too much, tap out," said Cassidy. "It's fine."

"Shall we get comfortable, then?" asked Deacon.

Cassidy pulled down the strap of Tatum's dress,

licking her shoulder. "Yeah, because I need to see her out of this…strapped down and begging for it."

Tatum smiled, turning to Cassidy. "Maybe it's you I want strapped down."

Cassidy licked his lips, palming his dick with no shame. "I'll do whatever you want me to do, mama. Tonight is for you."

Miles kissed Tatum on the temple. "Baby doll, why don't you get yourself refreshed? We'll be out here. Waiting for you."

"Good idea." Tatum finished her drink, placing it on the bar. She eyed the bartender, who simply gave her a wink. She headed toward the bathroom. "I'll be back. When I come out, be naked. All of you."

"Yes, ma'am," they said in unison.

Tatum went into the bathroom and closed the door.

Dear God, was she really doing this?

She took a few deep breaths and stared at herself in the mirror. It's not like she hadn't had sex already with all of them, together and individually, many times at this point. But the energy tonight felt differ-ent. Charged.

Yes, I want to do this. Fuck, I want this. I want them.

Tatum opened a bottle of water from the counter and took a few sips. She fixed her hair back into place and reapplied her lipstick. She looked down at her hand and removed her wedding band, putting it in her purse. It was the first time she'd taken it off since Frankie died. She slipped out of her dress, leaving on her underwear because she knew that one of them would want to undress her. Just as she was about to step out of the bathroom, she felt her anal plug vibrate. Rapidly. Tatum stumbled a bit and held on to the counter, letting out a moan so loud that it felt like it shook the mirror.

Outside the door, she could hear Miles say, "Deacon, chill! You're gonna kill her before she's ready."

"I'm done! I promise!" Deacon chuckled. "I'm just keeping her on her toes."

Tatum walked out of the bathroom in just her heels and underwear. She gave Deacon a side-eye, but he just smirked. He went to the bench and picked up a black lace rabbit mask that covered half the face. He quickly tied it across Tatum's face, giving her a peck on the cheek. All three of them were naked, as she requested. Tatum walked around, giving each of their bodies a good perusal. Deacon leaned against the bar, Miles sat on the bench in front of the bed, and Cassidy lay across the bed. Their dicks were all semi-hard as they stroked at various rhythms. Knowing that all three of them were there for her gave Tatum a rush of arousal and power.

"So, who's going to eat my pussy first?" asked Tatum as she sat on the bench facing all three. She opened her legs and plunged her fingers into her panties, stroking her folds as she looked at them. She took a wet finger out of her pussy and pointed. "Is it you, Cass? Or you, Deacon? Miles, perhaps?"

All three men stood, making their way to the bench where Tatum sat. She grabbed a mask and placed it on each of their faces. Seeing them in these black *Phantom of the Opera* style masks turned her on even more. It was as if she was fucking total strangers. Cass and Deacon both sank to their knees. Miles sat next to her, removed her bra, and began tweaking her nipples between his fingers. She then placed her wet fingers into his mouth, and he licked greedily.

"You can have us all, darling," said Deacon as he crooked a finger in the elastic of her panties.

Cassidy pulled down the other side. "We can take turns. I've always been good at sharing my toys."

"Good boys," said Tatum as she ran her fingers through Deacon's curls. Deacon lifted her left leg over his shoulder while Cass lifted the right one over his, licking the inside of her thigh. There was a slight height difference, but Tatum adjusted by leaning back on her elbows. Luckily, the bench was wide enough to accommodate her body.

Deacon parted her pussy lips with his fingers and moaned. "Fuck, it's so pink and pretty." He dove in, licking her slowly, sucking her labia and flicking her clit occasionally. Tatum dropped her head back and Miles was there waiting, his lips and tongue connecting with hers. She moaned into his mouth, aroused by the syncopated rhythm of Miles' kiss and Deacon's licks.

Deacon gave Tatum's pussy one last kiss, moving out the way to let Cassidy take his turn. Cassidy went straight for her clit, lifting the hood with his tongue and latching on, sucking with a fury. When he added a thick finger to the party, Tatum lost it.

"Oh God, Cass!" Tatum tried to reach for his head but Deacon and Miles held her hands down. Deacon and Miles both took a nipple in their mouth, sucking and nibbling. Little tiny fires burned across her skin. She could do nothing but take the assault on her body as orgasms began making her feel like she was having an out-of-body experience.

"Look at this pussy. Wet as fuck. I thought you said you didn't get that wet anymore?" asked Cassidy, who wasn't really looking for an answer. Instead, he kept up his steady attack on her G-spot with his thick yet nimble fingers and more-than-capable tongue.

Tatum whimpered, unashamed. She wanted to

clench her thighs but she couldn't. Deacon and Miles held onto them, spreading her legs wide open as she sat. She could only let her wetness drip with abandon down into Cassidy's thick beard.

"She doesn't have that problem with us, now does she?" said Deacon, taking a finger to sample a trickle of Tatum's juices off her inner thigh.

"Never. We keep that pussy wet," whispered Miles in Tatum's ear, licking the shell, sending a shiver down Tatum's spine. "And you're right Cassidy, she looks so good plugged. Stretching her asshole out for us."

"For you," Tatum panted as she came down from the last orgasm. "Only for you."

Tatum rested for a few beats before she stood up and walked over to the X-cross. The pulsating rhythm of the music piped into the speakers beat in time with her chest as she touched the straps and inspected the apparatus. Deacon and Miles were leaning up against each other and Cassidy had his hands behind his head as he stared at her. They were all waiting to see what she'd do. Would she let them do the things she'd only fantasized about?

She looked over her shoulder at her men. "I'm ready."

❧

Deacon positioned Tatum facing them in the X-cross, making sure the ankle and wrist restraints were secure.

"Remember your safe words," Miles reminded her before placing a kiss on her lips.

As Deacon oiled Tatum down, she watched through her mask as Cassidy picked up a riding crop and Miles picked up nipple clamps. Just the thought of those on her body made Tatum anxious and ready to feel them.

Deacon walked around to marvel at his handi-work. "You look so divine up there, Tate. Like a work of art."

"She does," Cassidy said as he rubbed the riding crop over her breasts and down her stomach. "Like a living, chocolate doll. A doll I want to punish." He gave Tatum a slight swat against her nipple and she hissed, the sensation sending shockwaves to her pussy. She forewent a gag because she wanted to make sure they could hear her safe words if she wanted to tap out.

Before she could recover from the sting of the crop, Miles placed the nipple clamps on her, giving them a slight tug. The sensation made her breasts feel full and heavier by the seconds.

"Your tits look so good this way," said Miles, and

he kissed Tatum on her neck as he gave them another tug. She moaned, throwing her head back.

"Oh no," said Cassidy. "You don't get to come yet. You will not come until we're balls-deep inside you. Understand?" He gave her a swat to her thigh with the crop.

"Yes, Sir. I won't come."

"Good girl, Tate." Cass rubbed the area where he'd hit and placed a kiss there for good measure. When she looked down at him, he winked. A rough and sweet teddy bear. That was Cass.

Deacon approached her, licked his fingers, and drove them into her pussy. He curled them, pressed against her spot, and activated the vibration in the anal plug simultaneously. Tatum's legs shook. If he didn't stop, she was going to come all over his hand.

"I don't know, she seems wet right now. Look at that pretty face. She is begging for us to let her come."

"Please," Tatum begged. "Let me come. Please, Sirs."

Deacon kept going, pumping his fingers in and out, seemingly hoping that she'd create a wet mess on his hands so he could punish her. "Should I let her come, fellas? What do you say?"

Tatum was so close to coming that she could cry.

Cassidy tugged his lower lip between his teeth,

his eyelids heavy with desire. "Absolutely not. She gets to come when we say so." With that, Deacon pulled out his fingers, which were soaked. He licked one, then stopped.

"Miles, I think you should have a taste." Deacon placed his fingers into Miles' mouth and Tatum watched as he sucked off her juice like it was the most expensive Beluga caviar. It nearly unraveled her.

Miles released Deacon's fingers from his lips with a moan. "Damn, Deek, that tasted good. I need to thank you for that, baby." Tatum chest heaved and her clitoris thumped as she watched Deacon and Miles exchange a deep, near-sloppy kiss. Knowing that they were tasting her juices between their tongues drove her insane.

"You like that, don't you?" said Cassidy, as he stood in front of her. She watched as he stroked his dick to a painful hardness, precum leaking from the tip. "You're ready to be fucked, aren't you, mama?" Tatum dropped her head. She couldn't look at Cassidy. She felt a slap of the riding crop to her clitoris and nearly screamed.

"Look at me. I asked you a question. You want to be fucked, don't you?" Cass' words were harsher, gruffer. This only made Tatum wetter and more impatient.

Miles pulled at the nipple clamps. Tears rolled down Tatum's cheeks. "Answer him." Miles turned the X-cross to face more of the two-way mirror. "Do you want those people out there to watch you get fucked?"

Cassidy gave Tatum's clit another swat, and that was it. She yelled and screamed at the top of her lungs, each inhalation of air burning them.

"Yellow, sir! Yellow! Yellow!"

Deacon quickly untied her and placed her on the bed. He rubbed her sore nipples, placing gentle kisses on them and rubbing her clit. The bartender brought over electrolyte drinks. Tatum drank, catching her breath. Deacon moved to place Tatum's head in his lap.

"How are you feeling, darling?" asked Deacon, running his fingers through Tate's hair.

"Great, that was amazing." Tatum smiled.

Cassidy kissed Tatum's shoulder, giving her soft rubs. "Let us know when you're ready for more. Take all the time you need."

Miles dropped to his knees and licked and sucked her pussy, easing the sting from the riding crop. "Better, love?" he asked with a smile and a glistening beard.

Tatum rubbed his bald head. "Much better."

She paused as she looked up at the three hand-

some faces staring at her. "But I need to feel you...
All of you... inside me." The "all of you" wasn't
directed at Miles' alone, and they knew it.

Miles got on the bed and positioned Tatum on
top of him. He eased his dick inside her pussy, not
moving yet, simply pulsating inside her.

"I think that ass is ready," said Cassidy as he
pulled the anal plug out slowly, replacing it with the
tip of his dick, already coated in lube. Slowly, he
eased the mushroom head of his dick into her and,
once in place, Miles and Cassidy pumped inside her.

Tatum was speechless at the feeling of them
both. Cassidy rubbed her clit from the back, slapping his heavy sack against her ass. Deacon watched,
rubbing his dick until he was so hard that he was
nearly purple under his dark skin.

"Where's my dick?" Cass asked, showing no
mercy to her gaping asshole as he drilled inside her.

"In my ass, oh God!" moaned Tatum, feeling the
pleasant burn and stretch of him.

"Whose pussy is it?" asked Miles, who was
keeping up stroke for stroke.

"Yours," Tatum growled as sweat trickled down
her neck into her cleavage.

Deacon moved on the bed, leaning down and
taking one of Tatum's nipples into his mouth. Still
sore from the clamps, when Deacon's teeth grazed

her nipples, Tatum let out a strangled moan. She gripped Miles' shoulders, trying to hold on as Cassidy inched deeper inside her ass. She pulled Deacon up from the bed and was now eye level with his dick. Without warning, she took him in her mouth and sucked.

"Fuck," was all he could yell as Tatum slurped, licked, and let him fuck her face. She gagged around his dick, spit and precum dripping down her chest and onto Miles' torso. She was consumed with need and lust. She wanted them to claim her, to leave their mark deep inside her. She wanted to feel them all come in every available orifice that she had. The Tatum before Franklin may not have felt this or wanted this. She felt new, and most of all, free. Free to express desire however she wanted to. In some ways, Franklin had given her the permission to do so.

She could feel Miles jerk first, coming into her pussy. He didn't move as he watched Deacon come into Tatum's glorious mouth, his dick covered in remnants of red lipstick. She opened wide, taking in every drop that he had and swallowing it. Deacon bent down to kiss her, then fell onto the bed. He then kissed Miles, wiping sweat from his brow with tender, loving care.

Cassidy grabbed Tatum's hair, fisting it until he

let out a roar, painting the walls of her ass with his white-hot cum. Tatum received every drop, savoring the sensation inside her.

Once Tatum came down from the orgasmic euphoria, Deacon brought over alkaline water for all of them. Tatum drank as Miles brushed strands of hair out of her face and Cassidy rubbed her calves. They were a mess of tangled limbs in the bed, their chests still heaving and breathing still ragged. Despite the music, Tatum could hear the sounds of people outside, reacting no doubt to the performance the four of them just put on.

"I wonder if they enjoyed the show," Tatum asked out loud.

Deacon shrugged. "Doesn't matter if they did or not. Did you enjoy it, honey?"

"I did. But..." Tatum bit her lip, feeling guilty about craving more from her guys. They needed breaks. They weren't spring chickens. She knew they could keep going too.

"Just say it, Tate," encouraged Cassidy. "All we can say is yes or no. Although, we'd be hard-pressed to say no to you."

Tatum licked her lips, looking between Deacon and Miles. "I want to watch you two fuck."

Deacon raised a brow as he looked over at Miles, who rubbed his chin with a smile.

"Actually, it's been a minute since I've been in that ass of yours, Deek," said Miles. "Wondering if you still feel as good as you look,"

Deacon swallowed, shaking his head. "I wouldn't mind that at all. If Cassidy is cool."

"Do your thing," Cassidy nodded. "Besides…" He licked Tatum's inner thigh, and she moaned. "I'll find something to occupy my time with."

"Actually, I'd like to occupy myself with Tatum too," said Deacon as he began stroking himself back hard.

Miles gave Deacon a look of recognition. "Ah, I get it. But can you handle that?"

"I can always handle what you bring." Deacon gave Miles a slow, tongue-heavy kiss that made Tatum wish she were in the middle of it. She loved watching them kiss. They had their own rhythm that she couldn't match. It was truly a secret language.

Cassidy began kissing Tatum's shoulder, moving his lips to the curve of her neck. "You like it when they kiss, don't you?" Tatum nodded, her eyes transfixed on Miles and Deacon. They were on their knees, kissing. Miles' hands reached down to Deacon's dick, stroking it with precision. Deacon gritted his teeth between strokes as if Miles' firm grip was almost too much for him to bear.

Deacon threw his head back, his jaw muscle flexing. "Fuck, Miles, don't make me come yet."

Miles didn't stop his strokes. Instead, he taunted Deacon. "You see what you do to him, Tate? Do you want Deek to fuck you while I fuck him?" asked Miles, not looking in Tatum's direction.

"Yes," Tatum breathed out. Her back arched off the bed as she felt Cassidy's lubed-up fingers inside her. He stroked her until the sloppy wetness of her pussy was the only sound they could hear.

Miles stopped stroking, grabbing Deacon's head as he licked into Deacon's mouth. Deacon moaned, a response Tatum was all too familiar with. Having been kissed by all three of them, Tatum enjoyed Miles' kisses the most. He was an amazing kisser.

Cassidy pulled his fingers out and licked them. "She's ready for you, fellas. Aren't you, mama?"

"Yes, please." Tatum was now begging, her voice cracking on each syllable. "I need you to fuck me, Deacon."

Deacon and Miles broke away from their kiss, turning their attention to Tatum. They each honed in on a breast, kissing and sucking on her nipples until they were taut.

"Remember, honey, you still have safe words," said Deacon as he licked the underside of her breasts. "If things become too much, we will stop."

Tatum nodded, but she knew they'd revved her desire up to ten. There was no way she'd stop this. She wanted it too badly.

Deacon positioned himself at her entrance, running his dick up and down her slit, coating himself with her juices. Tatum's muscles contracted, almost wanting to suck his dick inside her. As Deacon pushed in, he let out a loud groan, as if he hadn't been inside her many times.

"Fuck, every time I'm in your pussy, it's so good. So right." Deacon pushed Tatum's legs open wide as he thrust inside her. Just as she was about to scream, Cassidy planted his lips on hers, sucking her bottom lip until she was gasping for air.

Tatum could only breathe as Deacon's thick, veiny dick hit all the right spots. As Tatum felt an orgasm coming on strong, she dug her nails into Deacon's biceps. Deacon relished the pain, smiling as Tatum's nails were close to drawing blood.

"Don't make her come yet, not until I'm inside you," said Miles, who was close to Deacon's ear, licking the side of his bearded face. In what seemed like a millisecond, Deacon lifted himself off of Tatum. She whimpered at the absence of him, but Cassidy was there to make up for it. He slid down between her legs and sucked her clit, making her shudder.

"I'm going to come, Cass," she begged. "Please let me come."

Cassidy smiled against her wet, needy pussy. "Soon, baby girl. I'm just getting you ready for your ride."

No sooner had Cassidy said that, Tatum looked over. Miles was on his back, his wet, lubed up dick angling for Deacon's ass. Deacon straddled him, reverse, as he adjusted to Miles' dick.

"Come here, darling," grunted Deacon, extending his hand to Tatum. "Come ride me."

Tatum was concerned. Could Miles handle all this weight on him? But her concerns were voided once she climbed on top of Deacon and he took control.

"Holy fuck," she cried as the feeling of Deacon's dick was multiplied by the feeling of Miles underneath him. Deacon held on to Tatum's waist, pushing deeper into her as Miles' pushed deeper into his ass.

"God, your ass. I've missed this," said Miles as he thrust into Deacon. "Tell me how good Tatum's pussy feels."

Deacon neared euphoria being between Miles and Tatum. "Fuck, you two feel so good. Shit." He grabbed Tatum by the throat, applying pressure as he thrust deeper inside her. "Tate's pussy is addictive."

Tatum was about to come as her walls tightened and juices dripped down Deacon's dick. Their bodies were sweaty, nearly overheating with each touch—each thrust. She was sure that if she felt one more orgasm, she'd be joining Franklin in the afterlife. But she would not tap out. She would not call "red" anytime soon. Bliss was taking over.

Cassidy was at her side, giving her kisses on her lips. "Look at my girl, taking this dick like the boss bitch she is. It feels good, doesn't it?"

Tatum nodded. "Yes, oh God, yes."

"You want them to come, don't you?" asked Cass, who reached between Tatum and Deacon, finding her clit to stroke it.

"Yes, fucking yes!" Tatum was losing her grip on reality, her eyes pooling with tears as the next wave of orgasms hit.

"Good, princess," Cassidy gave Tatum another long, deep kiss, then pulled back off the bed. "You heard what she said, fellas."

Tatum felt Miles still underneath them. His grunt was so unrecognizable that it was startling. He slowly pulled out of Deacon's ass, but still took the weight of Tatum and Deek on top of him. Despite not being filled with Miles, Deacon kept thrusting inside of Tatum. She held on, gripping Deacon's wrists until she came hard.

Miles stroked Deacon's balls until Deacon let go inside of Tatum in several quick, hot spurts.

Tatum lifted herself off of Deacon and lowered her head to lick between the two of them, tasting a mix of their respective juices on her tongue. It was heavenly. Just like mix of their essence, Deacon and Miles seemed better together than apart.

Tatum hoped they realized that.

Cassidy's dick was practically leaking in anticipation. Once Tatum had her fill of Miles and Deacon, Cass pulled her toward him, kneeling over her as he aimed his dick at her breasts. In a fury, he came all over her tits. He rubbed his cum over her breasts until he was satisfied.

Cassidy stared at the scene before him. "I wonder how all of us taste at the same time. Why don't you tell me, doll?" With that, Cassidy took his cum-soaked finger and stuck it in Tatum's mouth. She greedily licked it off and moaned. All three of them on her tongue was a taste that she was growing fond of.

Completely spent, all four of them collapsed their sweaty and stained bodies onto the bed. Tatum lay her head on Cassidy's chest while Miles wrapped his arms around her. And as usual, Deacon was behind

Miles. She was sure to others they all looked like an odd group, but to Tatum, this was heaven on earth.

Miles stroked Tatum's hair, kissing her on the check. "What's next on the agenda, doll?"

Tatum stretched her arms, looking at the pure love and affection all three of them had for her. And she for them.

"Let's go home, baby."

20

CHAOS AND CONFUSION

The sun peeking through the blinds finally stirred Tatum from her sleep. She was tired and sore, but in the most pleasurable way imaginable.

When they returned to her place from their time at Secrets, they continued their sexual exploration in Tatum's bed. This time, things moved much slower, softer. Yet, they wouldn't stop until Tatum was left fully satisfied. Eventually, they all climaxed and fell asleep soundly, falling into their usual spots in the bed.

She stretched and felt around the bed. There was no one to the left or right of her. Worried, Tatum sat up and looked around the room. Had they all left? She threw on a robe, gargled a little mouthwash, finger-combed her now curly hair, and walked down

254

the steps and toward the kitchen where the smell of coffee and bacon permeated the air.

"Dude! Chill!" Deacon was at the stove, swatting away Cassidy from taking a piece of bacon from the sheet pan. Miles was at the kitchen island, reading on his phone and sipping coffee. Tatum leaned against the doorframe and watched the scene. It was so perfectly domestic. They looked so natural and comfortable there. All of them shirtless and in their boxers or briefs. Was this how it was going to be forever?

"Morning," she said, breaking her silence as she made her way into the kitchen.

"Morning, love." Miles met her halfway, kissing her lips. "Would you like me to fix you some coffee?"

"Yes, please." Tatum nodded and kissed Deacon on the cheek before sliding into the other chair at the island. She watched as Miles fixed her coffee just like she liked it. Two splashes of cream and two spoons of sugar. The first time he did that, she asked him how he knew her coffee order. He simply said, "I've known you for twenty-plus years. You pick up on things."

Cassidy came over to give Tatum a kiss. She tasted the saltiness from the bacon on his tongue. "You're going to eat today," he admonished. "Last night, you didn't eat enough. I was worried."

Tatum had been so euphoric and into the night, she hadn't really wanted to eat anything. Cassidy reminded her that part of aftercare was eating, so she had a few bites of cheese, crackers, and grapes. Still, it wasn't enough to satisfy a very grumpy Cassidy. He'd made her a PB&J when they got home. Under his watchful eye, she ate every bite.

"I'll eat, Daddy," Tatum smiled as she rubbed his bicep. "I promise."

"Calling me Daddy won't get you out of eating," Cassidy gave her thigh a light squeeze before heading to retrieve the dishes and silverware for breakfast. "You'll eat, mama."

"What's for breakfast?" Tatum sipped her coffee as she watched Deacon move about the kitchen, his back muscles on full display as he went about chopping and stirring. There was something sexy about a man who knew his way around a woman, a man, and a kitchen. Deacon looked over his shoulder and smiled.

"Your favorite. A spinach and feta frittata, bacon, and home fries with onions and garlic. And Cass is right, you can't sweet talk us out of eating. You're trippin'."

Tatum laughed, turning to Miles. "You're going to let them talk to me this way?"

Miles looked up from his phone and smirked.

"Absolutely. It's three against one. Besides, you're going to need your energy if you plan on handling all of us."

Deacon brought over a plate for Tatum, placing a napkin in her lap. "Open," he said to her, motioning with a forkful of potatoes. Tatum opened her mouth wide, savoring the taste of the home fries. "Deacon, you're a wiz with the cooking. And a talent behind the camera. What else can you do?"

Deacon leaned down, whispering in Tatum's ear. "You forgot to mention my talented tongue and dick too."

Tatum choked as she laughed. "Now, if I would have said that, two other people with those same talents would be jealous."

"We all have our skills," Miles laughed. "Some of us better skilled at the dick than others."

"Glad you recognize that," quipped Cass as he piled his plate high with food.

"Some of us better at taking the dick than others too," said Deacon, giving Miles a thorough once-over as he licked his fork.

Tatum looked between them with a sly smile. "Should I give you two some private time? It's cool with me."

"Now you already know," Miles slid a hand under Tatum's robe, finding her at the beginning stages of wetness. "It would be fun, no doubt. But not as fun if you weren't there."

Tatum bit her lip and moaned at the feel of Miles' long fingers between her wet slit. "Please stop, otherwise Cass is going to be upset that I didn't eat."

"Very upset," said Cass as he washed his frittata down with orange juice. "Let her eat, Miles."

Miles sucked his teeth, removing his hand from her robe. He licked his fingers and moaned. "But she tastes so fucking good, Cass."

They all laughed, talking over one another until they heard the thud of something hard hitting the floor.

Tatum turned to find Morgan standing in the kitchen next to the mudroom, his suitcase and duffle bag at his feet. His eyes were wide and confused. If Tatum could bury herself into the ground with Franklin, she would have at that very moment.

"What the fuck is going on here?"

Tatum tightened her robe and came close to Morgan. "Hi, baby. I wasn't expecting you for another week." She tried to pull him in for a kiss but he backed away. A look of disgust was plastered on his face.

"I came home early because I knew your anniversary was yesterday. I thought you'd be alone. But... what's going on, Ma? Tell me the truth!"

Tatum sighed. "It's not…not what you think!" Actually, it probably was exactly what he was thinking. He'd just walked in on his mother getting fingered at the kitchen island by his Uncle Miles.

"Oh, really?" Morgan folded his arms across his chest. "What's it like, then? Because it looks like you are having a fucking orgy with these men in my father's house!"

Tatum stared at Morgan wide-eyed. She'd never in her life heard him be so angry. "Watch your tone, young man! For your information, this house belonged to the both of us."

"Mom, you know what I mean! What are you doing? Dad's barely cold in the ground! Is this what you've been doing all summer while I've been in DC?"

Tatum sighed, reaching her hand out to Morgan, who backed away. "Let me explain, honey. Your father…"

"Don't bring Dad into this," Morgan interrupted. "Ain't no way to explain this. You're out here being a whole slut and my dad is dead."

"Hey, son," boomed Miles, coming to stand next to Tatum and putting an arm around her. "Watch how you talk to your mother."

Morgan, with his long legs, took three strides before he was in Miles' face. "Who the fuck are you talking to, Miles?" The way Morgan said his godfather's name made it seem like it was bile rising in his throat—gross, purulent, and disgusting.

Cassidy rose to his feet. "Morgan, you need to chill."

"Chill?" Morgan voice shattered into a billion pieces. "You expect me to chill and you're standing in my kitchen with a half-hard on? Dude, fuck you!"

Cass cleared his throat, quickly covering himself with his hands. "Your mom is a beautiful woman and…"

"Are you all trying to seduce her? Get her money or something? Why the hell are all of you half-naked?"

Tatum took offense to that. She wasn't some rich widow to be seduced. Clearly, she was in a robe. Everyone had on boxers. Well, Cass was barely in his briefs. Still, no one was half naked…exactly.

"Absolutely not!" said Deacon as he untied the apron that was around his waist. "We are here because we love your mom. We knew how hard yesterday would be for her. We didn't want her to be alone either."

"Love her?" The situation clearly confused Morgan as he rubbed his temples. "So, all three of you? On my parents' anniversary? Oh God, I think I'm going to throw up."

"Morgan!" Tatum called out to her son, but he flew past her and up the stairs to his room. She heard the door slam, tilting the photos on the wall. Tears welled up in Tatum's eyes. Tatum wanted to tell Morgan about this arrangement in her own time. She didn't want him to find out this way. Not with him walking in on them in various stages of undress.

Tatum turned to face Cass, Miles, and Deacon. "I think you all should leave. Let me talk to Mo."

Miles pulled Tatum in for a hug. "You sure? You don't have to do this alone. Let me talk to him."

Tatum looked up at Miles. Morgan had been closest to Miles, who he viewed as an uncle.

Tatum shook her head. "No... I'll handle it. He's shocked right now. I would be too if I saw my mother this way. Don't worry about anything. I'll clean up."

Miles let Tatum out of his embrace so that Cass and Deacon could both kiss and hug her.

"We'll grab our things," said Cass. "Call you tonight?"

Tatum shook her head. "No. Give me a little time. I'll call all of you later on. I need to talk to my son."

One by one, they came back downstairs fully dressed. They all kissed Tatum on the cheek before heading out. Tatum waited until the guys left the house to hit the back of the pantry and poured herself a shot of whiskey. She hated whiskey, but she needed some liquid courage to face Morgan.

Tatum knocked on the door to Morgan's room. She heard nothing, so she turned the doorknob to find it unlocked. Morgan was seated on the edge of his bed, his head in his hands as his locs fell all around his face. Tatum sat on the opposite side of him, putting enough space between each other that she didn't smother him. She placed a hand on his shoulder and Morgan stilled. He looked up at her with red-rimmed eyes and a red nose. Tatum's heart broke knowing that she caused his tears.

"Ma, please tell me you aren't doing what I think you are."

"Well," Tatum swallowed. "I can't lie to you."

"Oh god! Ma! Why? I mean, I get that sometimes people mourn in different ways after someone dies, but this is a crazy way to process grief."

"Look at me." Tatum took Morgan's hands and folded them into her own. "I am still mourning your father. But I need to explain something to you."

Tatum tried her best to explain Franklin's last wishes to Morgan, leaving out some things that she knew he wouldn't understand. He squinted through-out, as if his brain couldn't comprehend any of it.

"So, what you're telling me is Dad wanted you to be with his three best friends? My godfathers?"

Tatum nodded. "Yes."

"And they agreed to this? No questions asked?"

Tatum chuckled "Oh, they had questions, but they loved me and Frankie enough to honor his wishes."

"This isn't some sick attempt at just trying to fuck—I mean, sleep with—you, is it? Shit, how does it even work? It's one of you and three of them!"

Tatum rolled her eyes. "I would have thought my gay son would be more open-minded."

"Wait," said Morgan, wide-eyed. "Don't tell me that the fellas are getting down with each other too. Wow..."

Tatum would not put their sexual arrangements out on front street with her son. "Morgan, you sound very judgmental right now. And your father and I didn't raise a judgmental young man. I mean, I didn't judge you when you were barely nineteen and started dating Raheem, who was my T.A. You were barely a sophomore, and he was in graduate school."

Morgan waved his hands. "Ma, that is totally different!"

Tatum folded her arms. "How so? Raheem is nearly seven years older than you. I told you he was too old for you, but you didn't care. You said you were in love, so I let it go. If this were a heterosexual relationship, I'd have the same concerns. But I couldn't stop you then nor now. You're an adult. And so am I."

Morgan leaned back, giving his mother a hard stare. "You telling me you love them? All three of them?"

Tatum sighed. "I can't say that it is love. It's different. It's a mutual adoration and attraction. And Morgan, they truly will do anything for me. And you. Their word is their bond."

Morgan ran a hand through his locs. "Ma, this is the craziest shit—I mean, stuff—I've ever heard in my life. My mother in a quad with my godfathers. Insane. And how is this supposed to work? You all live together or something? Are they moving in?"

"Whoa!" Tatum held up her hands. "We haven't discussed that far ahead, but I am enjoying my time with them."

"So, how does it work? You go on dates with each of them? And then you all have group dates? Do the dudes have dates alone too?"

Tatum laughed. "Something like that. The fellas still play basketball with each other every week, just like when your dad was alive. But their time with me is different." Tatum looked at her son, who wore a pained expression. "But if this is causing you distress, I…we…can call this whole thing off."

"I think you should," said Morgan without

missing a beat. "You need to be focusing on yourself, your teaching obligations. Missing Dad. Not getting dicked down…dear God! I gag even saying it."

"Morgan Simmons!"

"Sorry. But Ma, this is crazy! You've got to admit that!"

"Fine," Tatum sighed. "I will call them and tell them this will not work. You're right, maybe I need to focus on other things."

Morgan kissed his mom on the cheek. "Good idea, Mom. Maybe we can chalk this up to some kind of lapse in judgement. A summer fling just to get your rocks off."

Tatum gave a weak smile. "Sure. Maybe it was like that." She rose to head out. "There is breakfast on the stove. Please eat something. You've had a long day already."

Tatum avoided Morgan for most of the day, electing to stay in her room. Her cell phone was full of unanswered messages. Some were from Nadine and Alisa, wondering how the rest of her evening went. The others were from Cass, Deacon, and Miles in their group chat.

MILES

Talk to me, T. You okay?

CASS

Hadn't heard from you in hours.
Need proof of life.

DEACON

An emoji would do. Something, Tate,
darling.

MILES

We can come back if we need to.

Tatum stared at the screen. Her eyes were so blurry with tears that her head hurt. She could barely see the words she was typing.

TATUM

I think we need to pause this.
Indefinitely. I've hurt and confused
Morgan. I need some time.

DEACON

You sure about this?

MILES

I can explain to Morgan that we
aren't trying to use or hurt you, baby
girl.

TATUM

I am sure about this. I said let's just
try this for the summer, didn't I?

MILES

You did.

DEACON

Well, I guess it's over with.

CASSIDY

K.

MILES

That's all you got to say, Cass?

CASSIDY

She's decided. Let her be.

DEACON

He's right. We have to respect Tate's
wishes. We love you regardless,
darling.

About a half an hour later, Tatum received a
separate text from Cassidy.

CASSIDY

You know I'm not one to talk about
my feelings like this. I am a man of
fact and science. But I care for you,
Tate. You are in my DNA now and I
can't shake you loose even if I tried.
Please don't end this.

Tears fell onto Tatum's phone as she stared at
Cassidy's words.

TATUM

I care about you too. But Morgan is
my son. I cannot hurt my baby and
appear to dishonor the memory of
his father, even though I explained to
him it wasn't like that.

Tatum placed her phone on the nightstand to charge. She pressed a button to lower the shades in her bedroom and got under the duvet. She sniffed her sheets, still smelling like parts of Deacon, Miles, and Cassidy.

She buried herself under the covers and vowed to not come out until she was exhausted from crying and every tear had fallen.

21

RESOLUTION

Fall semester was here before Tatum knew it. She was back to her regularly-scheduled life of boring department meetings, office hours, and classes full of fresh-faced and temperamental co-eds. She stared around her office and inhaled.

It was good to be back for a change. Maybe she could take her mind off of things. It had been weeks since she spoke to the guys or Morgan. She hadn't even told Alisa or Nadine the sordid details. Only that she'd ended things with the guys. Nadine said that maybe it was for the best. Alisa simply sighed and said, "I hope you know what you're doing."

As Tatum unpacked the last of her CLA journals, she heard a knock at her door. She wasn't expecting anyone, but she guessed it was probably some eager

269

freshman trying to get a jump start on brown-nosing. Instead, she was surprised to see Morgan at her door. After their discussion, Morgan had decided that it was best for him to stay with Raheem for the rest of senior year. Tatum didn't object.

Tatum looked up from her boxes. "I didn't expect to see you this semester."

Morgan walked in, hands tucked in his pockets. "I know. But I needed to see you, Mommy."

Tatum's heart nearly burst at Morgan calling her "mommy." She hadn't heard that in years. She motioned for him to sit but he waved her off, electing to stand.

"Mom, I came to apologize to you."

Tatum looked at him wide-eyed. "Honey, there is no need to apologize."

Morgan shook his head. "Yes, there is. I blew up at you and your choices. I talked to Raheem about this and he set me straight."

"Oh, did he?" Tatum folded her arms as she sat on the corner of her desk. "What did he say?"

Morgan looked down at his feet, shuffling them. Tatum smiled, reminded of his sweet kinder-garten self from long ago.

"He told me I was being an uptight ass. He told me to stay out of grown folks' business. Whatever arrangement you and my dad had is between the two of y'all. I had no say in how you coped with Dad's death, or what you did afterwards. You're an adult. I can't police your sexual habits."

Tatum gave a slight smile. "You know, I've always liked Raheem."

Morgan chuckled. Tatum extended her arms out for a hug, and Morgan clutched her. "I love you, Mom."

"I love you too, Mo.'"

"And if Uncle Miles, Uncle Deek, and Uncle Cass make you happy... and that's what Dad wanted... then I say let them make you happy. Just promise me something."

Tatum kissed his forehead as she ran her hand through his locs. "What's that, baby?"

"If you are gonna choose a step-daddy out of that bunch, pick Uncle Miles. He's the richest. No shade to Deek or Cassidy but I'd prefer a rich step-daddy."

Tatum let out a raucous laugh. "I am not thinking of marrying anyone, but I'll keep that in mind, baby. By the way, they are all rich."

Morgan frowned. "For real? Even Cassidy?"

Tatum nodded. "Especially Cassidy. He's a patent-holding astrophysicist."

Morgan's jaw nearly hit the floor in shock. "Seriously? I thought he was an assassin for years. Or a spy. Or even a drug dealer."

"Funny. I did too," Tatum laughed.

"Damn, and you think you know a person!" said Morgan with a smirk.

Tatum raised a brow. "I feel like that was low-key shade towards me."

Morgan kissed his mom on the temple and smiled. "You'll never know."

After the dust from the first weeks of classes settled, Tatum decided to reach out to Miles, Deacon, and Cassidy. She didn't have any expectations, but she did want to see them again and tell them about her conversation with Morgan.

She also missed them more than her heart could stand.

She asked them to meet her at Crowne and King at the Griffin Hotel again, not because she had an expectation of sex, but because she wanted a comfortable public setting and alcohol. Difficult conversations were always had over a fantastic cocktail.

Tatum looked in her compact again, making sure her lipstick wasn't out of place or that she wore too much blush. Maybe she'd gone overboard.

"You look beautiful, as always," a familiar baritone said as she looked at her reflection.

She looked up to find Deacon standing there, looking sexier than he had a right to be. He wore khaki shorts, showing off his amazingly toned legs and a denim shirt, rolled up to show off his very strong, corded forearms.

Tatum swallowed, motioning for Deacon to sit. He slid into the booth and kissed her on the cheek.

"I didn't expect you to be first. Miles is usually the timely one."

"Yeah, he had a late client but he's assured me that he'll be here."

Deacon ordered a whiskey neat and the two settled into casual conversation until Cassidy walked in. Tatum's eyes were stunned as she saw Cassidy clad in glasses and a tailored suit that looked bespoke. He was on full Dr. Valentine mode today.

"Wow, Cass, you look great," said Tatum as he slid into the booth. Cassidy placed a quick peck on her cheek and gave a slight smile.

"I know you haven't seen me in full Dr. Valentine mode before, but I had a presentation for a job interview."

Tatum furrowed her brow. "A job? Where?"

Cassidy bit the inside of his lip. "We can talk about that later. I need a drink." He signaled for the waiter and ordered a rum and Coke. "Where is Miles?"

"Meeting with a client," explained Deacon. "He should be here soon."

Tatum ordered a martini and they all sipped their drinks in relative silence until Miles showed up. He'd gotten rid of his jacket and tie, coming in with rolled up shirt sleeves and navy slacks. He looked exhausted.

"Sorry I'm late. Difficult client," said Miles as he slid into the booth next to Cassidy.

Tatum waved her hand. "It's fine. I understand. I'm just glad you all decided to meet me. Do you want to order a drink first, Miles?"

Miles shook his head. "I'll stick with water for now. Saving the liquor for later if I need it to nurse a broken heart."

"Miles!" admonished Deacon. "Stop being so fucking dramatic."

"Whatever." Miles rolled his eyes and continued to sip his water.

"Okay then." Tatum gave a tight smile. "Well, I guess I better get this over with." She took a sip of her martini and took a deep breath. "I had a talk with Morgan. At first, he was angry. He felt like we were dishonoring the memory of his father by being together this way. He also thought I was

going through some sort of sexual mid-life crisis."
Tatum chuckled and the guys relaxed. "Nevertheless, after some soul-searching and reflection, Mo realized that he had no business judging this arrangement. Especially after I told him that his father was the one who wanted this for me. And…I want this."

Miles nodded. "Does he realize we aren't trying to replace his dad? I loved Frankie." Miles voice broke as he said those words.

Cass gave him a firm shoulder rub. "We all did, Miles. Real talk."

Tatum grabbed Miles' hand across the table. "Absolutely, I assured him that we aren't doing this for any nefarious reasons other than we care about each other."

"We'd never hurt you," said Deacon, putting his arm around Tatum.

"Because we love you," said Cassidy. "Shit, I'm in love with you."

Deacon nodded as Miles smiled. "He's not lying," Miles said. "We do love you."

"I love you too," Tatum smiled. "Even though he said it was cool, I know my son. It's going to take him some time to get used to this arrangement."

"So, what do you wanna do, T?" asked Cassidy. "It'll hurt, but I respect your decision."

Tatum nibbled her bottom lip. "I don't want to hurt you all."

"But?" Deacon asked, brows raised.

Tatum smiled. "That's it. And I don't want to end this. This summer has been the happiest I've been in ages. I spent nearly two years miserable, waiting for my love to die. And now, I get to love three amazing men. I'm blessed. It's not just the sex… It's everything. The way you all care for me is something I know I can't, and won't, get anywhere else."

"So, you're not leaving us, Tate?" Deacon pulled Tatum's hand up to his lips as he planted kisses. "Because I don't think I can bear it."

Tatum smiled, tears pooling in her eyes. "I couldn't either. Frankie asked you all to be with me for a reason. And I understand it fully. You all love me in all the ways he did and all the ways he wanted to continue doing. You just picked up the baton. Besides, I can't date anyone after this."

"Good." Cassidy pulled Tatum by the chin and kissed her deeply, her lips parting for him. "You're ours. No one else's."

Tatum turned to Miles, who hadn't said much. He stared into his glass of water. "Miles? What's wrong?"

Miles looked up and gave a slight smile. "Nothing. I came here prepared to walk away from this.

From you. I was pissed. Angry that you'd throw this away when it was just blooming. But who was I fooling? Cass is right. You're ours, baby."

"So, what's next?" asked Deacon.

Tatum took a deep breath. "Well, I say we keep doing us. And we don't have to explain our situation to anyone. The people who really love us will understand. Mo will come around eventually."

"True," said Cassidy, lifting his glass toward Tatum.

Tatum leaned over to kiss Cassidy, then Deacon. Finally, she stood and leaned across the table and to kiss Miles. With the softest touch, he smiled against her lips.

"Hi," he said.

"Hi," Tatum said, giving him another peck.

"Alright you two," said Deacon with a chuckle. "Y'all save the love fest until after we have some dinner."

"Actually," said Tatum, with a sly smile. "Our suite is available tonight. Maybe we can just order room service."

Cassidy downed his glass of rum and Coke. He stood, extending his hand to Tatum.

"Let's go, baby girl. We've got some lost time to make up for."

"Most definitely," agreed Deacon who stood next to Cassidy and Miles.

Tatum looked up at her guys. She was indeed a lucky girl. She grabbed Cassidy's hand, and then Deacon's.

"Let's go."

EPILOGUE

1 YEAR LATER

*T*atum lounged on her chair reading the latest Nnedi Okorafor book. She enjoyed the feel of the Mexican sun on her skin and the salty breeze of the Caribbean Sea. Miles rented the private villa in Playa del Carmen for two weeks instead of one. He insisted that they get there early to just be alone before the wedding festivities got out of hand.

Miles and Deacon were in the swim-up infinity pool. Tatum watched them playfully splash water on each other, kissing and laughing in between. It took this unusual arrangement for the two of them to realize that perhaps there was something more between them than just the physical, and that they had been denying a love that was slowly blossoming between them. After twenty-plus years, it was the slowest burn ever, but totally worth it.

Tatum's phone buzzed. She put her book down and read.

"Guys, Morgan and Raheem have landed safely. They are at baggage claim. They are getting on the private shuttle in a minute."

"Finally," said Cassidy, who was beside her in a lounge chair reading the same book. "I was getting worried when we hadn't heard from them." He removed his shades and looked at Tatum with a frown. "Don't tell me you've read past chapter 16 already. This is supposed to be a buddy read, you know? We read at the same pace, then discuss. Or did you forget how that works?"

Tatum laughed. "Chill, Captain Planet. Don't be mad at me because you read slow as a turtle." She turned to reach for her sunscreen, but Cassidy took it from her, motioning for her to spin around so he could reapply. He unstrung her bikini top so he could apply the lotion to her back unrestricted. He moved her goddess braids to one side as he began to work his magic.

"You're very good with your hands, Dr. Valentine," purred Tatum as she leaned into his touch, enjoying the coolness of the sunscreen against her skin.

"You already know that, Dr. Simmons," Cassidy said, placing a kiss on her shoulder.

"Maybe I wanted to put lotion on Tate!" yelled Miles as he swam up to the edge of the pool. Tatum watched as the water rolled off his body, glistening on him like flecks of gold. In his white trunks, he looked like a Grecian god. He pulled himself up and sat on the edge of the pool.

"You snooze, you lose," said Tatum. "Besides, we still have a whole week left of lotioning me up. Is that a word?"

Deacon swam and sat next to Miles. His hair was shorter and grayer now. "Actually, we don't. Morgan has us ripping and running all week for wedding prep. As groomsmen, we kind of don't have a choice in the matter."

"What could he possibly need?" Tatum rolled her eyes. "I wish he would let Alisa do her job as planner and coordinate everything. She's been running around making sure things are all set."

"And Nadine," interjected Deacon. "She left that sweet EJ at home to run Eddie ragged just to be here as extra hands. Mo needs to let them help."

Cassidy sighed. "Isn't Alex his 'best woman,' too? She can help him instead of sitting out by the pool hitting on the waiters."

Miles laughed. "Well, Mo is like Frankie in that sense. A total control freak."

Everyone laughed, but Tatum gave them a faint smile.

"Hey," Deacon placed a wet hand on her leg. "He's here with us in spirit, Tate. Don't be sad, my darling."

"Fuck!" Tatum sniffed back tears. "I'm trying not to, but it's hard. He really should be here."

"But we're here," Cassidy said. "What did we say? We are here for you and Mo. Period. We definitely weren't going to miss one of the biggest days of his life."

"I know," smiled Tate. "You never have."

In the year since they had been together as a group, the guys never missed a birthday or special occasion. They celebrated Cassidy's appointment as head of the astrophysics department at Tatum's university. At first, Cass thought she'd be totally against it, making their relationship awkward, but Tatum was beyond thrilled. Cassidy was the first Black man and youngest head of a STEM department at the university. It was a big deal. He and Tatum celebrated privately all across her desk in her office—another added benefit of them being colleagues.

All of them showed up to Morgan's graduation. Miles gifted him a brand-new Maserati as a graduation present. Tatum tried to object, saying that it was too lavish, but he wouldn't hear it.

"Nothing is too lavish for my boy," said Miles. Miles didn't stop at the car. When Morgan announced that he and Raheem were getting married and moving to DC for law school, Miles said that he'd pay for the entire wedding. Tatum quickly realized that Miles' love language was gifts. For weeks, he'd been sending them real estate listings for larger homes, something all four of them could be comfortable in. Although Tatum wasn't ready to part with her house just yet, she appreciated Miles' commitment to being with them all for the long haul.

They all celebrated Deacon's first major exhibit a few weeks ago. He'd taken a step back at the law firm to pursue his photography full-time. He'd done a gorgeous retrospective on Blacks in STEM, including some photos that featured Cassidy, gold grill and all. While everyone loved the photos, the guys agreed that the best photos Deacon took were in his private collection—the pictures of Tatum. He'd since added photos of Miles and Cassidy to the mix, some with Tatum, some solo shots. All in various stages of undress or ecstasy. Those wouldn't be in a gallery anytime soon.

"In the meantime," Miles said as he moved his

hand up Tatum's leg. "You need to relax as the gorgeous Mother of the Groom. Tell us what you need? A massage? A margarita?"

"More tacos?" laughed Deacon. Tatum smacked his arm. She had been inhaling tacos since they got there, but she'd also been burning the calories nonstop. If it wasn't an excursion to Tulum, or jet skiing on the ocean, then they were holed up in their villa, getting their sheets as sweaty as possible.

Tatum looked at all three of her guys, two of which were glistening wet and one who was all shiny with sweaty tattoos and ripped muscles. God, she was lucky as hell.

"I can think of a couple of things." Tatum finished removing her top and laid back. She felt three sets of eyes bore into her.

"Damn." Miles lifted Tatum's white-painted toes and began to lick them thoroughly. "I'm loving Vacation Tate. She's insatiable."

Deacon pulled at a string of Tatum's bikini bottom. "Me too, Miles. She's nastier, I think. I love it."

Tatum's laugh echoed. "I highly doubt that, but if it's true, it's your fault. All of you."

Cassidy pulled at the other string on Tatum's bikini bottom until he completely removed it. "Less talk, please. I'm trying to fuck this beautifully shaved pussy."

Miles rolled his eyes as his lips moved up Tatum's calf. He wasn't a big fan of the total bareness of Tatum's pussy, but he got outvoted when she asked. It didn't stop him from eating her out every chance he got on this trip.

Tatum was now completely nude, lying on the lounge chair. She had to chuckle to herself because it wasn't the first time she'd found herself in this position on this trip. She opened her legs wide, revealing her pussy to her damn-near ravenous audience. She rubbed her clit, enjoying the feel of her touch, her men, and the warmth of the sun on her deep brown skin.

"Look at you, our chocolate doll," said Deacon as he licked her hardened nipple. "Fucking exquisite."

Cassidy moved Tatum's hand away from her throbbing clit. "Let me handle that for you, mama." He took over stroking her swollen bud, which made Tatum writhe in the lounge chair. Cassidy had her number. He'd learned how to make her come within a matter of minutes.

"You've ruined me," moaned Tatum as she was coming all over Cassidy's hand. She was a messy, panting, overstimulated puddle in his hand.

"No, baby doll, you've ruined us," chimed Miles, who was licking the moisture of Tatum's leaking pussy from her inner thigh. Miles removed his trunks and pulled Tatum toward him. He was exquisitely bronzed by the sun, down to his dick. He opened her legs wide and pushed inside her. He pumped so slow—agonizingly slow—inside her, as if he wanted to relish the moment of being with her despite the fact he could have her again anytime he wanted.

Deacon jerked his dick as he kissed Miles. "Look how gorgeous your dick is inside her, babe. I'm so jealous."

"Don't be," Tatum moaned as she dug her nails into Cassidy's biceps. "Come here, love."

Deacon pulled down his trunks and rubbed his precum-leaking tip over Tatum's lips. She licked it off greedily and parted her lips to receive his concrete-hard dick. She sucked and slurped, filling her throat to capacity with Deacon as he thrusted his hips toward her mouth.

Cassidy licked up Tatum's neck, whispering his version of encouragement in her ear. "Suck the fuck outta his dick, Tate. Gag on that shit, mama." Tatum did just that, until Deacon was coming down her throat with a roar. She was thankful that they were fairly secluded, otherwise the scene they were making would have been damn illegal.

Miles was so close to coming, his face contorted and his forehead sweating. Tatum grabbed his waist and pushed him deeper inside her. "Come for me, Miles." She ran her nails down his back, cupping his ass. Miles shivered all over until he was releasing inside her.

Cassidy groaned at the sight. "I need to get in that pussy before you tap out."

Before she could catch her breath, Cassidy flipped Tatum onto her knees, and sunk himself inside her. Tatum moaned loudly, adjusting herself to the feel of his girth. Her pussy was dripping with Miles' cum, leaking all over Cassidy's dick. The sound of it was completely obscene and turned Tatum on to the highest. Out of the corner of her eye, she watched as Deacon licked off the mix of juices from Miles' dick. It was all too much and not enough at the same time.

"I love you," Tatum panted, gripping the lounge chair.

"I love you too," grunted Cassidy, placing a kiss on her lower back as he slammed into her.

"Love you, truly," said Miles as his fingers ran through Deacon's silver-flecked curls.

Deacon released Miles' dick, leaning over to kiss Tatum. "Love you more."

Tatum's heart nearly burst with happiness. She was convinced that this was heaven on Earth.

And she had her beloved to thank for it.

AFTERWORD

A New Nom-de-Plume. A New Adventure in Romance.

I have many people to thank for this "experiment" in writing that has brought me joy for the past few months.

First, I'd like to thank my groups, Inclusive Romance Project and Wordmakers for the encouragement.

I'd like to thank AH Cunningham, the queen of polyam romances, for her guidance in writing **The** Oath.

I'd like to thank my "tamer" alter-ego, the real captain of the ship, Tati Richardson, for letting **me** come out and play. This was a fun adventure.

More things to come…or should I say…cum… ;)

Lastly, I'd like to thank the readers, friends, and supporters on TikTok, Twitter, and Bookstagram who really encouraged me to stretch my writing muscle and try something new. I hope that this book made you horny and happy. If so, then I've done my job.

Love and Lust,

TM Richardson

9 798218 351083